GIRL OVERBOARD

GIRL OVERBOARD

SANDRA BLOCK

UNDERLINED

Text copyright © 2022 by Sandra Block
Cover photos: image of girl © 2022 by Carolyn Lagattuta/Stocksy;
boat deck and background © 2022 by Gabriel (Gabi) Bucataru/Stocksy

Visit us on the Web! GetUnderlined.com

Educators and librarians, for a variety of teaching tools,
visit us at RHTeachersLibrarians.com

Library of Congress Cataloging-in-Publication Data is available upon request.
ISBN 978-0-593-48346-6 (pbk.) — ISBN 978-0-593-48347-3 (ebook)

The text of this book is set in 11.5-point Baskerville MT Pro.
Interior design by Jen Valero

Printed in the United States of America
10 9 8 7 6 5 4 3 2 1
First Edition

To Margaret and Joseph Long
With love

CHAPTER

one

DAY 1

Departure

"Listen," my mom says.

I've learned that when she says this word, you should, in fact, do the exact opposite. *Listen* means a lecture is coming whether you like it or not, and steadfast ignoring is usually the best course of action.

"Your father and I work very hard to be able to afford nice trips like this," Mom continues. "And the very least you could do is . . ."

Blah, blah, blah, blah, blah.

Yes, I know they work hard. My mom's a lawyer. My dad's an actuarial accountant (which means people pay him a lot of money to tell them when they're going to die). And yes, I do appreciate how hard they work. But I'm not the one who wanted to take a stupid cruise to Bermuda in the first place. I would have been happy to stay home and hang out with Luke for spring break, which would have been . . . hm, I don't know . . . *free*. Then I wouldn't be stuck waiting in the arrival lounge, which smells of body odor and perfume, watching my annoying (though admittedly cute) toddler-brother while passengers scavenge the cheese-and-cracker tables like they've never seen food before.

"Okay?" my mom asks, sounding irked.

Which means the lecture must be over.

"Okay," I answer, even though I'm not entirely sure what she just said. But it seems to appease her, because she huffs out a thank-you and then stomps off to the reception desk to join my father, who's having an intense discussion about his lactose intolerance with the chef.

My brother, Trey, tries to escape the minute she turns her back, as usual, and I snatch him by the shirt that's stained with ketchup from the plane. Midway through the trip, he somehow found a handful of ketchup pouches. Our seat looked like a crime scene, and the stewardess smiled and said "no worries," but swore not-that-softly under her breath on her way to get more napkins.

"Go!" Trey complains, straining against my clutch like a puppy on a leash. He doesn't say that much, but when he does, it's with spirit. "Go!"

"I know, Trey-Trey," I say, springing up from my sitting position and knocking over my lacrosse stick, which had been leaning on the wall. I brought it with me on the cruise to practice, but it'll probably collect dust in the closet like usual. I suck at lacrosse but whatever. It's better than PE. "I don't want to be here either." I tousle his caramel-colored, curly, soft hair, and he gives me a look and puffs out his cheeks. The cheek-puff is a definite precursor to a full-blown meltdown, which we do *not* want. I glance over at my parents, who are gesticulating madly to a man in an apron. (Though I wouldn't think lactose intolerance would be that difficult to describe.) Trey's breathing elevates and his cheeks flush, which means we are approaching throw-yourself-on-the-floor tantrum stage. I bend down, stretching the bruise from where I tripped over Ursula, this Amazon of a ninth grader who swears she was just defending the crease but knocked out my breath nonetheless. "You want a lollipop?" I ask.

His crestfallen expression perks right up, and he gives me an excited nod.

"Is that a yes?" I ask, since the speech therapist told us to push him to use his words. He nods again, probably thinking I must be an idiot. *What did you not understand about my nodding?* His cheeks start to puff again.

"Right. I guess that's good enough," I say, digging through my purse for a cherry-red sucker, which should pair nicely with the ketchup stain. My mom will be all over me for giving him too much sugar, but he'll be her problem by then.

Trey plops down on the floor and starts noisily sucking, quenching his sugar fix. I join him on the scratchy carpet, a hideous royal purple with yellow pineapples, which carries a soft mildewy scent. As I pull up my legs, my shorts gap against my skinny thigh. I hate how bony-thin I am. My best friend, Miranda, says I have thin privilege and shouldn't "cater to the male gaze" anyway, so I should just shut up about it already. She's probably right. But I'm not, like, *pretty* skinny. I'm toothpick, mosquito-bite-breasts kind of skinny. And she's kind of chunky but, like, sexy chunky. And even if she doesn't care about the male gaze, she has awesome breasts with actual cleavage, so maybe she should shut up too.

I examine my bruise, the gross blob of yellow and purple crawling over my thigh like an octopus. Earlier this week, Luke's fingers were there, swirling above my knee but not daring to go any higher. The memory gives me a weird fluttering in my stomach, and I push on the bruise to make the quivery feeling go away.

Trey cocks his head, and with a sticky finger, pushes on the bruise too.

"Hey," I say, "don't." I swat his hand away when he reaches again, and I can see him considering a tantrum over this injustice but letting it go. He's got a sucker after all.

When my mom saw the bruise, she frowned, asking where I got it. I told her the truth, but she took a step toward me, her face all earnest and said, "If someone ever hurts you, you can tell me. You know that, right?" Annoyed, I assured her it was seriously the Amazonian Ursula, but she still side-eyed me.

We both knew "someone" meant Luke. For some reason, she hates him. No, the bruise wasn't from him.

But if she knew what we did before the cruise, she would hate us both.

I stand up to make this thought go away. Again, I check my phone, as I've done a hundred times since our flight landed, checking and checking in an endless loop. Luke still hasn't texted me. I sent him hearts and smiley emojis on the bus ride over, trying to say I love you without saying I love you, or at least without appearing totally desperate. If I'm honest, that's

4

another reason I don't want to be stuck on this cruise. We've only been going out since February. He said he likes me "a ton," but we're still in that early stage of official dating, where things could kind of go either way.

As my parents finally wind their way back to us, I spy a girl leaning against the wall a few feet down, sitting on her backpack. Her pink hoodie is pulled over her head, silky blond hair spilling out like a ruffle. Her parents tower above her, saying something I can't hear, but the tone is clearly peeved. She looks as bored as I do, with similarly boring, lecturing parents. Finally, she stands up and spits out, "Fine."

Looking at her, I can see she's pretty skinny, her jeans tight, her sweater hanging off her body. She probably has a million TikTok followers and a YouTube channel. Out of nowhere, she turns to me, and I'm about to look away when she surprises me by smiling. I smile back. She tilts her head toward her parents, while simultaneously rolling her eyes. I give her a nod of understanding.

"All righty," my mom says, approaching. She glances at Trey's sucker and wisely says nothing. "Our rooms are ready." She and my dad do a fist bump–explosion type thing, which couldn't possibly be more embarrassing. "Are we psyched?" she prods me.

"Yes," I say, standing up, "we are *psyched*."

"Listen," she says, again giving me the cue to put in my earbuds. The sound flows in from midsong, where I paused it on the bus ride from the airport. The Weeknd croons into my ears, and I think of last weekend, kissing Luke. After practice, we were leaning against a brick wall, the day cold, smelling of mud. He tried to unsnap my bra, and when I wriggled and said no, he sighed, seeming kind of annoyed.

"Not with all the people here," I said. Then he smiled, like he approved of the explanation at least. And I shouldn't need his approval, especially now, after I promised I would take the pictures for him. But his smile still made me shine inside. We kissed some more, and when we were done, my hands were shaking.

I think maybe I'll let him go a little further next time.

Maybe.

———

Our cabin is windowless and gloomy.

The designers tried to cheer it up with an LCD porthole window sporting animated ocean waves and bobbing brightly colored fish. But somehow, this embellishment makes it even more depressing.

"Okay," my mom says, forcing cheer into her voice, while surveying the basement cave we'll be occupying for the next ten days. The furniture consists of one queen bed and a crib, which partially blocks off the entrance to the minuscule bathroom. It reminds me of the tenement housing tour we took in New York City last year.

"Ha," my mom says when I voice this observation out loud. "Right. Tenement housing but with running water, room service, theater, and an all-you-can-eat buffet. Very similar."

I suppose she has a point. Then I notice something else. "Wait. Where am I going to sleep?"

"Oh yeah," she says, as if just noticing the fact that she owns a daughter. "The cot should be coming any minute."

"A cot?" I complain.

She raises one eyebrow. "Anyway," she says as Trey climbs onto the bed and tries unsuccessfully to bounce. "We won't be spending that much time in the room. We'll be sitting by the pool and hitting the beach."

Yanking open the closet nearest me, I thunk my lacrosse stick against the wall, then sit on the floor and glance at my phone again. No text from Luke. Maybe I put too many hearts on the last one.

"Hey, hon," my dad says from the corner of their bed, his nose buried in the hefty ship's manual. "They've got a macramé class you might like."

"Cool," my mom answers. "Sounds like fun."

Right. Sounds like the worst thing ever. I glance at my phone again.

"Izzy," my mom says, catching me in the act. "You know you can't check that on the ship once we get going, right? We'll get a thousand-dollar phone bill."

"I know. I know. I know." Since she's told me approximately a thousand times. "We still have like an hour before we go."

"Okay," she says, her point made. She peeks into Trey's pants, since he's newly toilet-trained. Her overgrown bob drapes her face, the mahogany brown stippled with silver threads. "You know, instead of pining over this Luke, why don't you go have some fun? We're about to sign Trey up for the Guppies."

7

Trey opens his eyes wide. "Guppies!" He slithers off the bed. "Guppies, guppies!" I think we are seeing a lollipop sugar high.

"You should check out the Hang Out," my mom says. "I saw some kids over there already."

I roll my eyes.

"Or just sit here and feel sorry for yourself," she says, her voice swerving straight from faux cheerful to aggravated. "You choose."

"Hey, hon," my dad says. "Looks like they have a Rockettes-style show tonight."

Tucking my phone into my pocket, I stand up from the floor. "Yeah, I think I will check out the ship a little bit."

Because if I don't get out of this room, I might just murder them both.

CHAPTER

two

The girl is there.

I figured she'd be too cool to venture into the aspiration-ally named Hang Out, a place that looks like it's trying too hard to be glam, with mood lighting; curvy, mod purple couches topped with oversize silver pillows; and black bean-bags strewn all around. Of course, the room also features the mandatory foosball table and video game consoles. Two boys have already claimed those, which is fine by me. This is one point on which I actually agree with my mom: video games are an absolute waste of time.

"Hey," the girl says when I catch her eye.

"Hey," I answer back, shocked that she's even talking to me. In school, it's just me and Miranda—the geeky girl and the gay girl. It's not like we're bullied or anything; just awarded benign neglect. In real life, no one who looks like this girl would ever deign to spend any social capital on me. "I saw you earlier," I say. "With your parents."

She shakes her head. "Not my parents. My aunt and uncle."

"Oh," I say, worried I've messed up already. Maybe her parents died or something.

"Anyway," she says. "I'm Jade."

"Izzy," I say. I think about shaking hands, but when she doesn't reach out, I keep my hand in my pocket. "What grade are you in?" I ask.

"Sophomore," she says.

"Same," I say, though I thought she looked a bit older.

As if reading my mind, she says, "I'm sixteen, though. Since I'm stupid and had to repeat first grade."

"Oh," I say, back to monosyllables, and give her an awkward nod. "Where are you from?" I ask.

"New Jersey," she says. "You?"

"Chicago," I answer. We seem to have run out of topics then. Checking out the room, I spy a cute guy lounging on one of the beanbags. He's your typical blue-eyed, blond-haired Viking type with ridiculously handsome genes, strong jawline, big shoulders, the whole thing. A football player, maybe. He looks older than seventeen to me (which is the upper limit of the Hang Out age group). Engrossed in a tablet, he hulks over the beanbag.

"Bryce," Jade says.

"Huh?" I turn back to her.

"The fine-looking boy over there," she says, tilting her head.

Caught out, I smile. "You've met him?"

"Briefly," she says. "Just to see if he's worth the time."

"Uh-huh." If she's serious, she is way more advanced at this stuff than I am. My go-to move would be to walk over, remain silent, and hope he sort of likes me. Jade drifts toward the C-shaped pleather couch. When she sits down, I follow.

"You have a boyfriend?" she asks, her knee bopping up and down.

I nod.

"Really?" She looks surprised, which I get. *A loser like you has a boyfriend?* Sometimes I don't believe it myself. "Pics?" she asks.

"Um." I dig into my pocket for my phone. "Yeah." I pick out one from our Valentine's Day dance. The whole thing was kind of stupid, with feedback on the sound system the whole time, and school-made soggy pizza. But it's also where we first started dating. We began dancing together almost by accident, as our friend groups commingled. He pulled me in to kiss him, and after that we were basically a couple. He smile-smirks in the picture, with his arm draped over my shoulders.

"He's cute," she says.

"Thanks," I answer, though I feel weird accepting the compliment. It's not like I had any part in his hotness.

A clapping sound emerges from the curlicue stairs. "Hey, everybody," a young woman calls out. Her hair falls in a splay of long braids. She doesn't look that much older than us. "I'm Leisha, and some of you have already met me. I'm glad you joined us at the Hang Out." She puts her hands on her hips. "I have a very special guest with us today." With a sweeping gesture, she presents a huge, bearish man with a broad chest in a stiff white uniform. His face is freckled, with a reddish goatee. He looks sort of like Van Gogh, if Van Gogh were a linebacker. "Captain Taylor . . . take it away."

He gives us a gleaming smile. "Leisha," he says. "Thank you for that fine introduction." He has a cheerful Australian

11

accent. I feel like he's going to ask us to "strike up the barbie" at any moment. "I'm so happy to have you aboard the *Crown Jewel*. But I just wanted to go over some very basic ground rules with you."

A muted sigh floated across the room.

"I know, I know," he says with an apologetic hand raise. Polite laugher follows. "Rule number one: no alcohol. We have a very strict twenty-one and over policy on our ship." He scans the room to make eye contact, and when satisfied, ends it with a staunch nod. "Number two: no drugs. I know marijuana is legal in many parts of the United States now, but it's absolutely *il*legal on the *Crown Jewel*. Yes? Okay?" We offer a few reluctant yeses, and he moves on. "Rule number three: no vaping. Again, a hard-and-fast rule." Jade sighs, and the captain seems to sense that he's losing the room. "And last but absolutely not least, rule number four . . . have fun!" He breaks out into another big Australian smile. "Okay?" He slaps freckled hands together. "Most important rule . . . really." He nods at Leisha then, his duty performed. "Now I give you back to your tireless leader. Thank you, everyone." With a brisk wave, he strides out the room.

Leisha exhales, with a thin smile that tells me the captain annoys her. "Okay . . . now that that's taken care of . . . who's up for an on-the-deck game of capture the flag?"

There is nothing I loathe more than capture the flag.

One of the boys pops up from the video console chairs. His name tag says "Caleb." He's a Black kid with a fauxhawk that's frizzy, orangish on top, his smile all braces. And he's almost as skinny as I am. His eyes dart around, perhaps reading the room to see if it's remotely acceptable to admit he wants to play. Bryce stands up from his beanbag with a groan. "I guess I will," he says.

The other un-name-tagged boy playing video games sighs. "Okay, I will too."

"You coming?" Bryce asks Jade while walking toward the stairs.

And so it begins . . . hot guy seeks hot girl. Tale as old as time.

Jade shrugs, searching my face, and I shrug back, though I would rather poke my eyes out, or maybe even take the macramé class. "Maybe next time," she says, perhaps reading my reluctance.

He answers with a pointedly noncommittal shrug, and they clamber up the stairs while we stay behind on the couch. "I hate capture the flag," I say.

"Same," she answers.

I give her a teasing smile. "It seemed like Bryce wanted you to play, though."

"Maybe. But I have a better idea anyway," she says, popping off the couch.

"What?" I ask.

"You'll see," she says.

And like a lapdog, I follow.

The smell of smoke pervades the casino, though no one is smoking.

Neon lights flicker everywhere, with brassy machines

offering up rows of cherries and money signs. Round, forest-green card tables dot the area, with splayed-out cards and bored-looking dealers. The din of beeping and dinging fills the air, the patter of coins falling into trays ringing out. The inviting sounds seem to say, *Come closer, here lies fun, spend your money.*

The guy checking IDs at the entrance turns his back for a second, and Jade flounces past him.

"I don't think we're allowed in here," I whisper, following her.

Jade gives me a grin that implies she's not big on rules. "We won't stay for long. Just want to check it out."

"Okay," I say, slinking behind her as she struts toward one of the tables. The room seems shady, with dim overhead lighting, despite all the neon and flashing lights. It's probably the only place on the ship (besides our stateroom) without windows. Perhaps they want you to spend hours in here without a sense of time passing, your money floating into the darkness. There's not much to see right now anyway—we still haven't left the dock. Reaching the blackjack table, I see stacks of maroon and black chips. The handsome croupier watches us with curiosity. He looks the part, with jet-black hair, black eyes, and a vest that strains against his muscular chest, pinned with his name tag. Diego. Jade leans an elbow on the shiny nautical wood. "Hi," she says.

Diego leans toward her with a playful grin. "You putting down a bet?"

She shrugs. "Maybe."

He touches the tips of his gelled hair, still smiling. "You seem a little young for that."

She leans down to flash some cleavage. Lure set. "Not that young," she says.

"Oh yeah?" he answers, his eyes running up and down her body. Lure taken. "How old are you, then?"

"Eighteen," she lies without batting an eye.

This time his smirk is less certain. "Yeah, right."

"Honestly," she says, almost purring. "I can show you my license."

Taking a chip off a stack, he rolls it between his fingers like a magician as he assesses her. "Either way, you have to be twenty-one to be in here without a parent."

We turn then as a man cheers, coins clattering onto a tray while envious bystanders crowd around to see. The wins are probably timed for the busiest shifts, the passengers salivating like Pavlov's dogs (a neurobiology factoid), lining up for more chips. *That could be me! That could be me!*

As the hullabaloo dies down, we turn to face one another again. Jade taps her white-painted nails against the glossy wood. "Actually," she says, "I'm not trying to gamble. I was just trying to see if anyone parties around here." She lifts an eyebrow.

Diego clears his throat. "Sure, they've got lots of parties on the ship. There's a Mexican night, I think. And the White Party is the big one."

She stares at him a beat longer. "Not that kind of party," she says.

A long pause follows as I watch the conversation like it's a tennis match. I'm not 100 percent sure what kind of party she's talking about, but I can guess it's the sort that Captain Taylor wouldn't approve of.

He puts the chip back down and opens his mouth to say something, when a juiced-up bouncer lumbers over to us. "Any problems, Diego?" he asks, with a name tag saying "Sergei" on his shirt. With his thick Russian accent, he could have been auditioning for the role of "mobster number three" in a movie.

"No," Diego says, sounding a bit cowed. "All good."

Sergei offers us a stiff nod; a steel-blue tattoo of a scythe peeks above his collar. His veins bulge out on his bull neck. A middle-aged man in flip-flops, board shorts, and a Mickey Mouse T-shirt bellies up to the blackjack table with a drink in his hand, though it's not even eleven o'clock.

A loud, low horn blasts a mournful sound.

"That's it," Mickey Mouse man says. "Ship's a-leaving." Then he turns to Jade. "You girls want a drink?"

Sergei steps in. "See you later, girls," he says with a patronizing toodle-oo wave.

Jade narrows her eyes at him, but we turn around. And through the sound of cards slapping on tables, and the crank of the one-armed bandits, we retreat.

CHAPTER

three

Dinner on the ship is pretty much just like dinner at home, with my parents ignoring me and begging Trey to eat. Of course, we don't have ivory tablecloths with gleaming silverware at home. We don't have a fading blue sky with miles of rippling ocean outside the windows (since we finally left the freaking port). Nor do we have four-course dinners, with the likes of escargot, beet salad, marbled steak, and a gelato sampler. Escargot are essentially garlicky snails, in case you weren't sure, and yes, they taste as bad as they sound. Trey dines off the kids' menus and pacifies my parents with half a chicken finger. I'm eating an overcooked salmon and dying to check my email, since Luke can't text me on the ship now that we're at sea. I tap the butt of my knife on the tablecloth until Trey decides that looks like fun and joins in. My mom shoots me a look.

I put the knife down. "Can I go check out the Hang Out?" I ask.

A thrilled smile pops onto her face. "Oh sure, of course."

I hate lying to her, but if I told her I was going to the computer center to check my email, she'd bring up Luke, and I don't feel like that lecture right now. Since I'm not even checking it for him. Well, okay, I am sort of checking it for him. But not just that.

"We might catch an act of the Rockettes show later," my dad says, combing his hand through his salt-and-pepper hair. He's beanpole skinny too, which is where I got my genes, I guess. My mom frets at her waistline and says she wishes she could eat anything and be that skinny. But she looks fine to me. "Maybe you can meet us," he says. "Trey is up for it."

"Hm," I say, thinking that sounds pretty tortuous. "Maybe."

I wend my way to the business center, a cramped room where a dozen or so internet-starved passengers hover over the computers. The place smells of new paint and Windex. I would just use my phone, but the speed sucks, even with the Wi-Fi, and supposedly, the internet is faster here. In any case, it still takes forty freaking minutes to get a seat, and I finally swoop into a chair and put in my code. I have to race to check my email within my ten-minute daily parentally allotted time. When I complained about this rule, I got a "listen, you're not going on a cruise to spend the whole time doing Facebook in your room." As if I would ever go on Facebook.

Impatiently, I wait for Google to fire up so I can get my Gmail. Of course it's taking forever, which eats into my time. I consider negotiating babysitting Trey into more internet minutes. But that would probably be met with "it's not babysitting, honey, it's just being a member of the family."

Finally, Google crawls onto the screen, and I get into my account. Scanning through my email, I realize I'm holding my breath. I see three new emails: one from Miranda, an entreaty to join Dungeons & Dragons club (in case I want to further socially ostracize myself), and penis-enlargement spam. My heart thrums, but I don't see anything else.

No one knows. Or if they know, they haven't told.

I release a relieved breath, but then also notice there's nothing from Luke either. I told him I can't get texts at sea, so he had to email. And he promised that he would write me "the minute I got on the ship."

I click on Miranda's email, which says "I love ya, girl. Have fun!!" paired with a goofy bon voyage GIF. "Miss you, love you back!!" I reply, and hit send, then notice I had only thirty seconds left and log off just in the nick of time.

————

Dejected from the utter silence from Luke, I go check out the Hang Out, figuring some other friendless losers might be in there.

But it turns out no one is *quite* as desperate or friendless as yours truly, because the room has been vacated, the glam purple looking tawdry in the harsh artificial light. I'm about to retreat back to our stateroom when I notice my name on the whiteboard.

> *Izzy,*
>
> *We're at the lido deck if you're bored.*
>
> *Jade*

The note surprises me and lowers my loser status by a couple points at least. They probably won't even be there anymore, but I make my way down just in case.

Walking down the stairs, my feet don't quite feel solid, still out of sync with the swaying ocean. It's like being on a moving walkway in an airport, where your feet don't quite have the rhythm of the spooling rubber floor. Passengers mill around, checking out the new digs they'll be inhabiting for the next week. Techno music spills out of the YOLO club, which has an eighties vibe, awash with mirrors and shiny black furniture. A line snakes around the 24-7 Caffeine Fix kiosk, where tattooed, white twentysomethings steam various forms of milk and call out orders. Finally, I get to the right floor. As I walk out onto the well-lit lido deck, the pressurized doors close behind me. The warmth outside seems to embrace me, after the aggressive air-conditioning inside. A soft hiss fills the air, and I walk farther to trace the source and realize it's the ocean, all those decks below us.

"Hey," a voice calls out. It's Jade. She's sitting with Bryce. Are they together already?

Of course they're together already; just following the natural course of Darwin's law, the fittest pairing off together. He reclines on a beach lounger, with Jade sitting between his legs on the seat. Her arms hang over his muscular calves. The blond hair on his legs shows up in the light. I can imagine touching them, the wiry roughness under my palms.

"Come over," she says, and I look up from his legs. She pats a chair next to her. Caleb sits on the other side, looking thrilled and amazed to be hanging out with the cool kids. I know the look. I've worn it. "Caleb was about to tell us a ghost story."

"Oh yeah?" I sit down, a warm breeze ruffling my hair and carrying a soft, salty scent.

"It's not a ghost story," he says, taking offense. "It's the truth."

"Okay, whatever," Bryce says. "Tell the story already." It sounds like there's already been quite the buildup.

"Fine," Caleb says, pushing up the sleeves of his gray hoodie. But then he pauses. "You guys absolutely sure you are ready for it?"

"Jesus Christ," Bryce moans, and Jade and I giggle at his grumbling.

"Okay, okay." Caleb leans forward in storytelling mode. "So, check this out. Supposedly, there's some kind of curse on this ship." Silence follows this statement. Then Jade chirps out a laugh. "No, really. I'm serious," Caleb says.

No one says anything for a second. "What kind of curse?" I ask. The question comes out too intensely, and everyone looks at me. I glance down at the deck to avoid the heat of their stares.

"People die," Caleb says, and when I look back up, he is staring right at me, his brown eyes shining in the overhead light. "People die on this ship."

This time, Bryce lets out a belly laugh. "Bullshit," he says, in a singsong voice.

"No, it's true," Caleb insists, inching forward in his chair. "It's well-documented."

"Well, sure," Bryce says, shifting his legs as Jade readjusts herself between them. "Like they might have a heart attack or whatever. But it's not like some mysterious curse."

21

"That's the thing," Caleb says, putting his skinny elbows on his skinny knees. "It's *not* some heart attack or something. They jump off the ship."

Jade sits up in the chair. "What do you mean? Like . . . suicide?"

"Maybe," Caleb says. "Or something else." He allows a dramatic pause this time, surveying us to gauge our attention. "Sirens."

After another pause, we all laugh, relieved. "Sirens?" I ask. "Like in the *Odyssey*?" Again, everyone looks at me, and my face turns hot. This is why I can't have nice things. Because I am a complete dork.

Bryce pulls a face. "What's that?"

"It's a book, you idiot," Jade jokes. "Izzy's smart and actually reads them." She says this in a way that rescues me from myself. I want to hug her.

"Yeah," Caleb says. "They're beautiful creatures that call out to people. Enchant them."

Bryce raises his eyebrows. "Enchant them so they jump in the ocean?"

Caleb shrugs. "That's what they say. But I'm not lying. People have jumped. Every other year for a while now."

"Every other year?" I ask, no longer worried about the story at all. I lean back in my chair, creaking the plastic straps. "They would have shut the ship down by now."

"Go ahead," Caleb says. "Google it."

"So, is this the on year or the off year?" Bryce asks, half playing.

"The on year," he answers. No one responds, but it's ob-

22

vious we don't believe a word. "You'll see," Caleb says. "I promise you."

"Uh-huh," Bryce says, and I lean my head back and stare up at the sky, glittering with stars. So many stars. An embarrassment of stars. I don't think I've ever seen so many in my life.

"I'm telling you. Mark my words," Caleb says, like some kind of wizard-preacher from a dystopian movie. "Someone will die on this ship."

The ominous words float over us like a curse.

CHAPTER

four

DAY 2
At Sea

I'm sitting with Jade at the Hang Out, killing time.

Today is the dreaded "day at sea," with nothing to fill the hours except the jam-packed pool and other boring enterprises like watercolor painting classes and shuffleboard. After breakfast, I do the only reasonably entertaining activity, checking my email. But even this depresses me. Still nothing from Luke. So, I made my way to the Hang Out, where I found Jade.

Jade lets out a gargantuan yawn when Hang Out baby-sitter Leisha appears at the helm of the room. "All right," she sings out, rubbing her hands together in anticipation. "Everybody ready for the big ping-pong game?"

"Oh yeah, I'm really good at ping-pong," Caleb says with enthusiasm. "You guys should see my spin."

I wince for him. Does he not realize this isn't something you admit?

"Yeah, I'm up for it," says Tom, a guy who's friends with

Caleb. At least I think his name is Tom. Truthfully, I don't have any real objection to ping-pong. There's not much else to do on the second soul-killing day at sea, since my dad's gone whiskey tasting, my mom's getting a massage, and Trey has been mercifully delivered to the Guppies.

"Why not?" I say. "I'm up for it."

"Okaaay," Jade says, like she's surprised. *The geek takes charge!* "Let's do it, then."

Bryce grunts, getting up from his too-small beanbag. Because wherever Jade goes, he will follow, as will Caleb. (Though, hopefully, he's not deluded enough to consider himself a contender in that race.) Once again, we ascend the spiral metal staircase, our feet clanking up and up and up until we reach the lido deck, all of us totally winded. Our group flanks the ping-pong tables. An elderly woman passes by us on the outside track, pumping her arms. She gives us a little wave with a gnarled hand. She's probably a hundred years old and could easily outrun me.

The ping-pong balls are dropped, with Bryce and Tom against Caleb at one table (since Caleb insisted that he should play solo), and me against Jade at the other. It becomes quickly clear that Caleb is as good as advertised and Bryce is competitive as hell. Meanwhile, Jade and I play a listless game, losing more balls to the ocean than completing volleys. Finally, Jade tosses her paddle to the middle of the table. "We done with this crap?"

"Absolutely," I answer.

"Good," she says. "Then I have an idea."

I stare at her. "Please not the casino."

"No," she says, flipping her hair out of her eyes. "No need. Diego's a douchebag anyway."

I assume this means he doesn't want to "party" with her, which is just fine with me. "Where, then?" I ask. "Your room?"

"Nah. My aunt and uncle are probably boffing right next door," she says, her face pinched in disgust. "They keep giving me hints like, *hey hon, you don't have to come back to your room for a while today, okay?* while giving each other these totally gross smiles."

"Ew," I say.

"Yeah, I know," she answers as we climb onto the elevator. We descend down to our staterooms on Deck Four. I've seen her room—windowless too. But at least she doesn't have a cot and a crib in there. We appear to be heading toward her door.

"I thought we *weren't* going to your room," I say.

Jade shushes me, whispering, "This is just in case, okay?"

I give her a clueless shrug, and she puts up a wait-a-minute finger. So, we wait, huddled against a wall. Finally, she plows down the hall as a cleaner emerges from a room, dragging a vacuum.

"Oh, awesome," Jade says with her most winning smile. "I forgot my key." An uncomfortable smile sits on my face, and the woman looks at us with suspicion.

"This your room?" she asks.

Jade answers with a decisive nod. The woman checks in with me, and I also nod, a little less decisively. "Seriously, we can call my parents if you want," Jade offers, sweet as honey.

"Forget it," the woman says with a shrug, probably

thinking she's got more rooms to clean and no time to spend on these idiotic kids. Humming some song, she moves on to the next room, and the door closes with us inside.

"What are we doing?" I loud-whisper.

The place smells of air freshener. Piles of folded clothes dot the room. Bottles of lotions cover every possible surface, with guidebooks spilled on the table and an expensive-looking pair of binoculars strewn on one of the chairs. Jade opens the minibar with the little dangling key and peers inside. "Score," she trills, sweeping the contents—a plethora of multicolored mini-bottles—into her satchel-purse. They clink together as she zips it up.

"Jade. What are we doing?" I repeat, though it's clear what we're doing.

She lifts her finger to her lips yet again, tilting her ear toward the door. I hear it too. Footsteps. We wait while my heart beats so hard it hurts my chest. The footsteps get louder but then pause. We both take a deep breath of relief, but then it happens.

We hear a key card sliding into the door.

Jade yanks my arm, and we scramble under the bed. The dust invades my nostrils, along with the smell of a wet bathing suit that somehow ended up there. We are both curled in a fetal position, jammed next to each other, our foreheads almost touching.

"Oh, I shouldn't have had that second plate of nachos. I am *stuffed*," says a female voice with a strong Southern accent.

"Free food, baby. Bring it on," a male voice says with the exact same accent.

I see large flip-flopped feet with chipped orange nail polish, followed by a pair of male feet with bunions. I sip little breaths so they can't hear me.

"Hey," the man says. "You wanna . . . get a little . . . busy?" His lewd tone allows no misinterpretation. Jade's eyes open wider.

No, no, no. Please God no.

"Hon, I'm too full," she answers. "Sorry. You wanna do the bird-watching thing?"

I start breathing again, and Jade shuts her eyes.

"Oh yeah," he answers, sounding unfazed by the rejection. "Let me just grab my binoculars."

"I think they're under the bed," she says.

No, no, I scream inside my head. *They're—*

"On the chair," he says, swooping them up. "Okay, let's get a move on. Starts in like ten minutes."

"Mm-hmm," she says, followed by the sound of stretching and bone cracking. "Oh, my neck is so stiff." Footsteps sound again, this time heading away from us. "Hey, wait a second." The chipped toenails stop. "Wasn't the key in the minibar?"

A pause.

My mouth goes dry. That's it. We're dead. We're busted, getting thrown off this ship.

"I don't know," the man says. "Let's go already."

"Okay, okay," she mutters. "Don't get your panties in a bunch."

"I'm not getting my . . ." The words fade as the door swings slowly shut. We wait there for a minute in case of a check back for a forgotten item. But only silence remains.

So we roll out from under the bed and open the door a crack, and Jade checks for them in the hallway. Once we're sure the coast is clear, we tear out of there and down the hall, her purse jingling with liquor bottles. We almost barge into a middle-aged couple at full speed.

"Hey, hey," the man says in a Southern accent. Binoculars bounce on his belly. "Be careful, girls, there ain't no fire." I check his feet, see bunions, and gasp, then we keep running until we get out of the staterooms area and into the vestibule by the elevator.

I can't help it. I start laughing, and Jade joins in.

"Oh my Gd," she squeaks through gales. *"You want to get a little . . . busy?"* she says in a near-perfect Southern imitation.

I am crying now, stamping my foot because I can't stop, and we collapse onto the floor, laughing so hard we can barely even breathe.

CHAPTER

five

Later that evening, we're in her room, all freshened up for the dumb magic show. We're both wearing ripped jeans and tight floral shirts, embarrassingly matchy, except that her shirt outlines actual breasts, while mine outlines a padded bra.

"You ready?" Jade asks, going over to the safe in the closet. "Time to get our stash."

"You put them in the safe?" I ask.

"Yup. Can't be too careful with the alcohol police," she says, tilting her head toward her aunt and uncle's. She types in the code, and the safe beeps. She scoops the mini-bottles into her hands. "Ten-thirteen, if you ever want one of them. It's my mom's birthday."

"Hey, that's my friend Miranda's birthday too," I say, then feel stupid. *Wow, Izzy, I bet she's so interested in your friend's birthday.*

"You go first?" she asks, laying the bottles out on the floral bedspread.

"Oh, sure," I say, trying to sound nonchalant, though my voice squeaks. I've had a sip of beer and peppermint schnapps once at a party with Luke, but I've never really been drunk.

"What do you want to start with?" she asks, sitting down on the bed and bouncing the bottles.

I study them, like I know what I'm doing. "This one," I say, lifting the brandy bottle.

"Damn, girl," Jade says, sounding impressed. "You don't mess around."

I shrug as if I do this all the time, and unscrew the top, which comes off with a tinny scrape. "Bottom-ups," I say, then feel stupid because it sounds like something my dad would say. I throw it back with a big swallow.

Which was a mistake.

"Hahhhhh . . ." My eyes fill with water. I have just ingested fire. "Hahhhh," I repeat.

"Yeah," Jade says, unscrewing the vodka. "I could have told you not to start with the brandy." She finishes the vodka in a couple sips like it's water. "Another?" she asks, pointing to the array of bottles.

I nod, but my stomach lining still feels scalded. I take a little longer to choose this time.

"Give it a minute," she says, sensing my misapprehension. She tilts her head back and forth, surveying the bounty, as if deciding on her candy bar at a vending machine. "Tequila," she says with some zest. She lifts the bottle in a toast, then says, "I'll just drink half. You have to try it."

"Okay," I say, my throat still raw from my brandy experiment.

She takes a big sip, then hands it to me, and I do the same. This one goes down a bit easier. "Now," she says, pulling two cans of Coke from her minibar (which I notice has been denuded of liquor, probably by her aunt and uncle), "we shall have a civilized drink."

I snort. "Which is?"

She pops open the cans, then pours the mini-bottle of gin into one, and another mini-bottle of gin into the other. She swirls them around a bit, and I suspect she's done this before. "Gin and Coke," she announces, handing me mine.

"How quaint," I say.

"Yes, very," she answers.

Then we sit on the floor, our heads leaning against the bed, and drink our sodas. The drink would be refreshing and tasty except for the alcohol, which kind of ruins it. Still, I know that's the point, so I force down another gulp.

Jade lets out an indelicate burp and takes another sip. "I used to be able to burp the national anthem," she says.

I clink my fingernails on the soda can. "We all have our talents."

She lets out a snicker. "You're funny. You know that?"

I can't help but smile at the compliment. Miranda says this all the time, but she's Miranda. "I try my best," I say.

There's a knock at the door, and I jump. "One sec," Jade says, popping up from the floor. She opens the door wide to her uncle with his walrus mustache.

"What're you girls doing?" he asks, leaning his head in and smiling widely.

I can just hear Miranda unloading on him, if she were here. *Girls? I don't see any girls here. I see young women, if you must use binary vocabulary at all.* For some reason, this makes me giggle. Jade shoots me a look.

"Hanging," she says in a bored voice.

I lift up my Coke can as evidence of said hanging.

"Okay," he says, though a note of doubt lingers in the word. The smile pops on again. "Don't forget, we have dinner, then the magic show. . . ." He consults his watch. "Dinner's in fifteen. And I gotta check on a few things beforehand so—"

"Yup," she says.

"We are ablaze with anticipation," I say. My mouth feels sort of funny.

Jade throws me another warning look, and the uncle gives me a half smile, his walrus mustache lifting. He backs away from the door, letting it swing shut.

"Your uncle is kind of weird," I say once he's out of earshot. I take a long glug of the soda, the taste growing on me.

"Yeah, I know," she says. "Marginally better than my aunt, though." She takes another drink.

"What's wrong with your aunt?" I ask, the words a little slurred.

She shrugs and takes another sip. "I don't know. She pretends I'm not there. Since she doesn't *want* me to be there."

I draw zigzags on the condensation of the can. "Why doesn't she want you to be there?"

Jade leans onto her side with a sigh. "You really want to know the whole boring story?"

I take another sip and shrug. "It's probably better than the magic show."

"This is true," she says, then swallows about half the can. "So . . . short version. Joanie and Bob Gibson, aka my aunt and uncle, never wanted kids. And Joanie's made me very aware of that. But—and get ready for the big plot twist—my mom's MIA so . . ." She points to herself. "Here I am!"

She gives me a self-deprecating smile, but it's a little shaky. "Where is she?" I ask quietly.

"Rehab, for the hundredth time. But this time," she says, her voice mock-stern, pointing an authoritative finger in the air, "it's court-mandated."

I crinkle my eyes. "Meaning?"

"Meaning," she says, her face losing all semblance of joking, "if she doesn't stay clean this time, she goes to jail."

I lean on my elbow, turning over onto my side too. "That's some serious shit right there."

"Yup," she says, taking another drink. "I told you it was a long, boring story."

"What about your dad?" I ask, my eyes feeling heavy from the drink.

"Who knows." She tucks a strand of hair behind her ear. "Never met the guy. Probably ODed by now."

"Oh." I don't say anything, feeling a beat of sympathy for her. My mom might be annoying and overbearing. But at least she's around.

"Anyway," she murmurs. "I just have to deal with it a little longer. Until my mom comes back." With that, she throws back her drink and lets out a truly majestic belch. "You ready for dinner?"

———

Our two families sit down together at dinner, with Trey in our stateroom with the Guppies babysitter.

This was my mom's idea, to get to know the Gibson family, "since you girls seem to be getting pretty close." I sense an ulterior motive, though—that she doesn't exactly love Jade and wants to keep an eye on us both.

"Hey, you guys look like twinsies," her aunt exclaims, immediately hitting on just what I hoped to avoid.

"Fraternal, though," I say, which is unnecessary. "But not like brothers." It hits me that I am totally drunk. Which is probably why my mom keeps giving me funny looks, while Jade seems barely affected.

"So," my mom says. Awkward silence follows. With quiet desperation, my dad flags down the sommelier. "Have you been on any other cruises?" she asks as my dad starts his nightly wine discussion.

Jade's uncle Bob looks uncomfortable in a wheat-brown suit and a button-down that strains at his belly. "First one," he says, smiling at Joanie.

So that takes care of that topic.

The sommelier returns, and wine is poured, though the aunt and uncle keep their palms over their glasses with a virtuous headshake.

"We thought it would be a good way to get to know Jade a little better," the aunt says, folding her doughy arms on the table with a docile smile. She smooths out her wrinkled lilac silk dress. Her mouse brown hair stays hair sprayed in place as she nods.

"Oh, that's nice," my mom says.

Jade stares ahead and blows a wisp of hair off her face. I can't tell if she's bored or fuming.

"Since we'll be spending more time with her," the aunt adds. "As a parental role model."

Now I spy a definite eyeroll from Jade. "I already have a parental role model," she says.

"You do," her aunt allows. "But . . . just until she gets on her feet again."

"Joanie," her uncle says, like a warning.

"Jesus Christ," Jade mutters, just as a group of servers comes by with appetizers.

The smell of escargot makes me queasy.

"Have you done the whiskey tasting yet?" my dad asks, trying to steer us back onto safer ground. "They really do a terrific job."

"Oh, no," Joanie says, with an apologetic look. "We don't drink."

"Oh," my dad says, blushing. "I didn't realize—"

"Don't worry," Joanie says, putting her hand on his arm. "It's just that addiction . . ." Here she drops her voice to a whisper. ". . . runs in the Gibson side of the family." She flicks her eyes toward her husband.

"Jesus Christ," Jade says, louder this time. Abruptly, she stands up.

Joanie leans back in her chair with her hand over her chest. "Where are you going?"

"I'm not hungry," she grumbles, putting her napkin on

the table. When I turn to get a better view, the room tilts in a disconcerting manner.

Bob gives his wife the briefest chastising glance. "Let's just enjoy dinner, shall we?" he says to Jade.

"I'm going to the cas—" She catches herself. "The Hang Out."

"Oh," Joanie says, pulling her chair back in. "To see that Bryce?"

So I guess that Bryce is her version of that Luke.

"Yes," Jade says, grabbing her purse. "I am."

But she's lying. If she's going to the casino, she's seeing Diego, not Bryce. And I don't trust Diego with a drunk Jade. Not for a minute.

"Okay," Bob says with a forced smile. "We'll save a seat for you at the magic show."

She gives him a look that says *don't bother.* I give her a look that says *please, please don't leave me here with them.* She mouths "I'm sorry" at me.

As Jade walks out of the dining room, we all stare at her empty seat in silence.

"The magic show should be fun," my mom says with a labored smile, her voice a couple of notes too high.

"Oh yes," Joanie says earnestly. "The entertainment has been top-notch."

Finally, the main dishes come out, steam escaping from under the domed metal lids. "Mmm." My dad theatrically licks his lips. "I'm starving."

A hot slab of salmon is deposited in front of me. The

smell wafts up, and my stomach heaves. I stand up. "Excuse me," I say in a panic.

My mom grips the arm of my chair. "Are you okay?"

I start to sit down again, but the smell attacks and I stand right back up.

"You look as white as a ghost," my mom says, her eyebrows knotted in worry.

I feel myself gagging and realize I don't have long here. "I have to——" I say, but don't bother to finish, tearing away from the table and making it to the bathroom just in time.

———

Needless to say, we miss the magic show, which is probably the only positive right now.

I stagger over to my bed, and my mom helps me get a fresh shirt on, since the other one was flaked with vomit. While my dad dispenses with the babysitter, I flop onto the cot, which lets out a high-pitched creak.

"Shh," my mom hisses. "You'll wake up Trey."

So I shush, staring at the mottled white ceiling. But then it starts spinning, so I close my eyes, afraid of vomiting again. I hear zippers unzipping, the soft scrape of clothes. Snippets of my parents' whispers float across the room.

Do you think it's seasickness? Or . . . I mean . . . she wasn't feverish. . . .

If I didn't know better, I would think she and that girl got ahold of some alcohol.

No, no. It's probably just the ship. She didn't wear the ear patch thing today.

I don't know about that Jade girl.

You're overreacting. I'm glad she made a friend. Remember the last cruise, how miserable she was?

Water rushes out of a faucet. A toothbrush scratches against teeth.

"Do you want any water?" my mom asks, the loud whisper hurting my ear.

I wave my arm around again, and thankfully, she goes away. After a while, I open and close my eyes to stop the room from spinning. It doesn't help. Lights click off, darkness descends. Spinning, spinning. The room falls quiet, and I can hear chirps of laugher in the room next door. Spinning, spinning.

I slip in and out of consciousness. Or maybe it's sleep. I'm not even sure right now. Minutes pass, maybe hours. But then something wakes me up, a loud chirp.

A bird?

The idea makes sense for about three seconds until I realize, of course there aren't any birds in our stateroom. My eyes open to the utter blackness of the room. Then the sound goes off again, lighting a square on the ceiling. A text.

My mom stirs, which reminds me that I shouldn't have gotten a text, since we don't have the free Wi-Fi package, and she'll probably get a million-dollar bill and ground me forever but . . . I reach over to the phone.

Miss you, babe.

From Luke. Finally, a smile takes over my face. Three little words. Maybe not "I love you," but I didn't expect that anyway. *Miss you, babe. Missyou, babe. Missyoubabe* . . . I feel my eyes closing, and I'm descending back into the spinning, but then the chirp sounds out again.

My eyes pop open, and I stare at the screen. Another message from Luke. I start smiling again, but then I stop.

Did you do it yet?

CHAPTER

SIX

DAY 3

Coco Island

The next morning, my parents drag me out of bed to go to Coco Island, which is basically a beach owned by the cruise ship company. Normally, I wouldn't argue with a beach, but today my head feels like it might explode, and my mouth still tastes dry and pukey, despite brushing my teeth about a hundred times. And my dad's exuberance isn't helping.

Woo-hoo!!! Beach time!!! You bringing your lacrosse stick, Izzy? We could play a little catch!

At least he's quieted down now that we're on the beach, with his book and enormously dorky earphones on. The sun beats down like a sledgehammer, directly hitting my head. I lie there on the bristly towel with a washcloth covering my eyes and sweaty forehead, wishing I could just die and get it over with.

"Hey," my mom says, nudging me.

I grunt out a response.

"You're gonna want to put on sunscreen," she says in her mom-voice.

"Uh-huh." I'm pondering how one could decapitate themselves and still live.

My mom leans closer to me. "Later, we're going to have to talk about what happened last night," she says.

"Nothing happened," I mutter. "I just didn't feel well." My words disappear into the towel.

"Uh-huh," she says. "I wasn't born yesterday, Izzy."

Luckily, I am literally saved by the bell, as my purse starts chiming with phone messages.

Messages are pouring in, so I sit up to check them out.

My mom looks up from slathering sunscreen on Trey. "Is that a text?" she demands.

"Hon, they have cell service here," my dad says, his head already buried in his phone screen, a full-blown addict getting his fix. In fact, all the newly dumped-off passengers appear to be hunched over their phones. It seems the cruise line did not only buy the island, but a satellite, too.

Forgetting all about my headache, I reach for my phone, chest tightening with anticipation. I whip through my email, but then blissfully see . . . nothing. Phew. No one has said anything. So no one knows.

For now. Pushing that thought away, I turn to my text messages.

"Go, go!" Trey says, trying to slither out of my mom's grasp.

"In a minute, Trey," she says, adding some last-minute dollops.

"Guppeeees," he whines.

"I know, I know," she grumbles.

Passing Luke's *Miss you, babe,* and less enthralling *Did you do it yet?* messages, I scan through more texts. One from Miranda: *Hey, girl, missing you in freezing Chicago! Hope you're getting sun!* And then, a more mysterious one from Miranda, sent last night around midnight. *Call me,* followed by another one at six a.m. *Call me please, when you get this.*

So she knows. She must know. Maybe she saw the pictures.

My forehead starts sweating again, the phone trembling in my hand.

Oh God, she must know.

"Hey," a voice says, and I drop the phone like it's on fire. I look up, squinting in the sun to see Jade.

"You look like crap," she says conversationally.

"I feel like it," I say, my voice still hoarse from vomiting all night. Jade, however, looks as fresh as a daisy in her white bikini. She plops down beside me. As she zips up her backpack, I get a peek of a purple paisley notebook with *Journal* embossed in gold script on the cover. I turn away, so she doesn't think I'm snooping. In the distance, I see Bryce's Adonis-like form and Caleb's rangy one playing frisbee in the surf. A couple other kids from the Hang Out are sunning nearby. Behind us, a huge tent has been set up for the cruise-sponsored "chicken barbecue" lunch. The nauseating smell floats toward us, along with noxious plumes of smoke. Just the thought of charred chicken makes me want to upchuck again. Near the picnic tables, their rubber tablecloths billowing in the wind, the mandatory steel drums play

"No Woman, No Cry," further contributing to my headache.

"Did you put on your sunscreen?" my mom asks, giving Jade a tight smile of hello. She has Trey by the wrist, who is trying to drag her over to the Guppies.

"Yes," I say. I did give myself a quick spray on the dock ramp. Since I'm naturally ghost-pale, I had to do that much. But I might as well get a tan out of this cruise if nothing else.

"I'm not the one who's going to get a sunburn," my mom warns, a stupidly obvious statement.

"I did, Mom," I grumble.

For her part, Jade kindly pretends not to notice our squabble. Then my dad spots someone serving drinks and starts singing the piña colada song.

I figure that's my cue to flee. So we go, and I leave my phone, with Miranda's messages and all its troubles on the towel.

———

Her voice undulates underwater.

"Amazing . . ." The word comes out garbled and warped.

But she's right, it is amazing. We're both floating, gangly creatures skimming the surface while brightly colored fish shoot underneath us. Snorkeling was Jade's idea, after we got sick of playing frisbee with the boys. All the boogie boards were taken, and the Hang Out scavenger hunt seemed lame even by Hang Out standards, though Caleb suggested a couple times that we should do it because he was "really good at scavenger hunts." But there was plenty of snorkeling gear, so we decided to have a go.

Jade signals downward. A pancake of a stingray glides by. I feel as if we're in another world, dangling in bathtub-warm salt water, time suspended. The sun cuts a ray through the water, lighting up particles, and the bubbles escaping from Jade's lips. She surfaces to get a mouthful of air, then submerges again. Her eyes look comically large in the mask, which is probably how mine look too. The bobbing waves hypnotize me as teeny slivers of silver fish move in a parallel array, pivoting together, fast and smooth as a blade. The ocean pulls me up and down, the sun beating on my shoulders. My eyes follow a flash of yellow fish. Spit pools in my mouth around the cracking sharp-edged rubber from the snorkel. I can hear my ragged, Darth Vader breathing.

In this world, there is nothing weighing me down.

No Luke. No Miranda. No secrets at all.

A tap on my arms breaks the moment. Jade points up with her finger, her legs scissoring beneath the water. I emerge, moving the snorkel off my face to hang from a strap on my neck. "You ready?" Jade asks, barely short of breath. Pink square marks from the mask ridge around her face. She doesn't bother with the snorkel.

"Okay," I say. I could stay here all day, though.

Slowly, we make our way to the shore, stepping on sharp stones on the way in. Foamy water swishes between my toes. Bryce waves at us from his paddleboard, the sun glinting off him like he's in a cologne ad. Caleb circles near him on a boogie board, his constant patter just audible from where we are. The tide carried us some way, and we're breathing heavily, plodding through sugary sand that coats our feet. Finally, we get to our scratchy white towels, each anchored down with our phones. Deliciously exhausted, we flop onto the towels. Jade combs her hair with her fingers.

My eyes sting with salt water, and the skin of my face is taut with it. A soft stinging creeps on my shoulders, probably the beginning of a sunburn, which means a torrent of *I told you so*s from my mom. I brush the sand off my arms that clings like a body scrub.

Jade's phone goes off, and she lifts it up and smiles.

Glancing at the number, I recognize the New Jersey area code, but then look away so as not to pry. We both lie down on our damp towels, staring up. Cerulean blue sky fills my vision, wisps of clouds like streaks of chalk. Closing my eyes, I feel just the barest tendril of a headache now. My breath slows, and I feel myself drifting off, when suddenly ice-cold drips of water shower over us.

I whip myself around to see Caleb shaking off like a dog. "Ugh," I say, frowning at his giggling.

"Not cool, Caleb," Jade says, cutting her eyes to him. "Not cool."

He folds his arms over his jutting rib cage, his expression abashed. "Jeez. I was just joking, guys."

Bryce sits next to Jade. She leans over and playfully nudges him, and he smiles almost bashfully. "Where's your paddleboard?" she asks.

He motions to a hut with his head. "Gave it back to the cruise people." He reaches over to scratch a spot on his back.

"Here," Jade says. "You're getting burnt." She pops onto her knees and grabs a sandy bottle of lotion. She squirts some on her hand, the bottle making a lewd farting sound. Inching over to him, she starts rubbing his back.

Caleb stares at them a moment, then clears his throat. "You want me to get yours?" he asks me. *If you can't be with the one you love . . .*

"Um, okay." I'm not dying to have his hands all over me, but I do need some more lotion, and there's no reason to be an asshole.

Cold lotion drips onto my skin, and he does a decent job smearing it around. His movements feel jerky and uncertain. But he works economically, not lingering in any spot, which I appreciate. "I think you're good," he says, and tosses the bottle into the sand with a thunk.

I lift the bottle up with a questioning look, and he says, "No thanks. I still got a lot."

His back *is* pretty coated with white. And I'm sure he'd rather have Jade working on him anyway. I'm a distant second to her, as he is to Bryce. We're like an SAT analogy question. Bryce leans forward as Jade kneads his back, his expression relaxed and close to blissful.

Right then, a shadow looms over us, the instant shade shifting the landscape of the moment. "Hey," Diego says, his hands resting on his hips. He has possibly an even better body than Bryce (though the contest would be close). A black tribal-looking tattoo marks his chest. Another one of a fish morphing into a mermaid swallows up his bicep and shoulder. I glance down, my eyes falling on his slip-ons.

Jade takes her hands off Bryce. "Hey," she says.

Diego runs his hand through his hair, his expression nervous. "I wanted to show you something. Over by the pier." He fixes her with a stare, not veering toward any of us for a second to include us in the invitation.

"Oh," Jade says, with what seems like a practiced air of surprise. "Okay, cool. I'll check it out."

I assume she knows what the mysterious "it" is, and also notice she doesn't ask me or Bryce to come, for that matter. Maybe this is what they were lining up last night, when she pretended to be going to the Hang Out. I assumed it has something to do with "partying." In which case, I don't know whether or not I wish she had invited me along.

"Back in a bit," she says over her shoulder. She trots off, and our eyes follow the figures walking away. Jade slaps his shoulder and laughs at something, and he puffs up his chest, laughing too. He throws an arm around her waist, and she doesn't remove it.

They disappear into the distance, and her absence throws a pall over our foursome, now a threesome. Caleb starts humming, maybe to mitigate the tension, but it only makes things more awkward. Bryce sits on his towel with a half-lotioned back, his injured fury hovering around us. I'm wondering if he thought they were exclusive, like, boyfriend-girlfriend. I sort of thought so too, though to be fair, Jade has never said one way or the other.

"Do you know what that's all about?" Bryce asks, trying to sound casual.

"Nope," I answer.

Again, silence fills the air. Caleb appears to be finding a Pandora channel. A cloud of barbecue smoke sails over, making my eyes water.

"Is she dating him?" Bryce asks me, his question coming off as an accusation.

I shrug, stunned by the questions, mostly because he barely talks to me. He turns then, pointedly staring at me, blue eyes lit up and angry.

"Seriously," I say. "I don't know."

Unsatisfied, he stands up with a grunt, brushing sand off his thighs with a murderous scowl. "Sometimes," he says, "that girl can be a real fucking bitch."

Then he stomps off.

And with a look of bewilderment, Caleb follows after him.

CHAPTER

seven

Staring at the carefully plotted row of palm trees behind the food tent, I stand on the gangplank, waiting. I am surrounded by sweaty tourists growing cantankerous with the wait to board the ship again. My bathing suit strap digs into my pink shoulder, which thrums with the unquestionable start of a sunburn.

After Jade disappeared with Diego, I waited for her like an idiot. Caleb went off to play soccer with some Hang Out kids, and Bryce checked in by my towel periodically, acting like he wasn't. But the main event, Jade, wasn't there.

A little kid jumps up and down beside me, bouncing on the plank, despite his mother's pleas to stop. A clownish red *O* circles his lips from a melting Popsicle. With his next bounce, I nearly drop my phone, and his mom yanks his wrist, hissing, *"Stop. It."* The said child starts wailing.

Since we seem to still be in a holding pattern, I call Miranda while I still have a cell signal and an international data plan. Her voicemail comes on.

Not here. You know what to do.

I clear my throat. "Hey, Miranda. Got your message.

Sounded . . . kinda urgent? Maybe not. Anyway. Miss you girl. Call me back. Love ya."

As I hang up, my phone chimes.

You are so hot, jelly belly. Can't wait to see you again.

From Luke. With heart emojis—actual heart emojis.

My heart jumps out of my chest. I bring the screen closer to make sure my eyes aren't playing tricks on me. A smile flies onto my face. *You are so hot* (!!!). I read the words again, a few times, savoring them. I want to hug them, taste them. *You are so hot. . . .*

I never saw Luke as the pet names type, so the jelly-belly thing seems kind of weird. But good weird, as in tilting toward solid girlfriend-boyfriend territory.

I miss you too!!!

Hitting send, I make the decision right then and there. I've been waffling long enough, and he's really not asking for that much. Just a little something to help him. Just this once.

I'll do it. I'll send him the photos.

———

The theme tonight is Mexican, and the dress code, "smart casual" (as opposed to dumb casual?), which essentially means no bathing suits. Trey wears his J.Crew model royal blue V-neck. My mom has on a sundress with jewels along the neckline, and my dad, his usual blue-button-down-and-khaki getup. I'm wearing white shorts and a shirt that my mom says is too tight, and my shoulders are sticky with aloe vera.

We make our way into the dining room, decked out with

sombreros and piñatas, and Mexican flag centerpieces on every table. The host greets us with an *hola,* while an obnoxious version of "La Cucaracha" plays overhead. Since the cruise has nothing to do with Mexico, this seems culturally insensitive at best. As soon as we sit down, Trey grabs a pair of maracas off the table, and my mom turns to me.

"Now, we have to talk about something," she says with a stern we're-about-to-have-a-lecture tone. For a second, I freeze. *Could she know?* But it's impossible. I didn't even send the pictures yet.

"About last night," she continues.

I sigh with relief, which she takes the wrong way.

"Yes, I know the last person you want to hear from is your mom. And I know you are testing limits, and all of that is healthy." This sounds straight from the *How to Raise an Independent Teenager,* hidden under the towels in her beach bag. "But I don't want you to fall in with the wrong crowd. Or make bad decisions, like I did in high school."

I blink at this statement. "Like *you* did?" I ask. "Wait . . . you actually did something wrong in high school?"

My dad chuckles. "Oh yeah," he says, dipping a chip into the salsa. "Your mom was quite the rebel." He leans over, as if letting me in on something confidential. "She once snuck out in Grampa's car to go to a concert." Then he pauses. "Age fourteen."

"Shut up," I say with a newfound respect.

"Right?" He nods, smiling at my reaction. "Oh, and wait." His voice grows animated. "Ask her about the time she picked the lock at her aunt's house so she could—"

52

"I *didn't* pick the lock," she interrupts, shooting daggers at him. "Let's not romanticize this, Ted."

"Oh, right." He sits back, appearing chastened. "Of course not."

Trey starts shaking the maracas. "Eat!"

"Soon, Trey," my mom says, rubbing her temples. "Ugh," my mom says. "I'm getting a ghastly migraine."

The speaker, now blasting "La Bamba," probably isn't helping either.

"Eat!" Trey repeats, sitting imperiously in his booster seat. He shakes the maracas some more. *Off with their heads!*

My mom grabs a bottle of ibuprofen that rattles in her purse. "Can I have a sip of your soda?" she asks. "I could really use some caffeine to go with this."

I hand it over, and she drinks half of it down in a gulp. Outside the window, the long gray ocean, rippled with waves, lies before us as we sail away from Coco Island.

"Eat!" Trey repeats. *Shaka-shaka-shaka.*

"Trey, be patient," my mom says, and I take out my phone, gazing at the words once more. *You are so hot.* I can't help but smile seeing them again.

I'm pathetic enough that I could stare at them all day.

"May I be excused?" I ask. My mom gives me a questioning look in response. "I want to go to the computer room."

———

When I get there, I notice one empty seat and take this as a sign.

More likely sent from hell than heaven, but I'll take it

either way. Grabbing the chair, I glance around, but everyone remains focused on their own computers. They don't care that I'm about to do something stupid. And bad.

But it will help Luke. And it's not such a big deal anyway.

My nerves jitter as I pull up my email and find the one that I sent to myself, with the attached photos. The thumbnails show the evidence. My hand hovers above the keyboard. All I have to do is forward them, and it's over. He said he'd never ask me to do it again. Just this one time, to help him out. The cursor rests on the forward button. I'm a second away from pushing it, when I feel breath against my ear, then a loud whisper. "Boo!"

I nearly jolt out of my chair.

"Dude," Jade says, laughing, but in a quiet voice. She perches next to me on the table. "You seriously need some Xanax," she whispers.

I put my hand over my thrumming chest. "You scared me," I whisper back, trying to sound nonchalant, though my voice comes out huffy. As my heart rate decelerates, I notice her hair—a mass of blond boxer braids. "Wow . . . those are . . ."

"Yeah, they took a while." We are speaking quietly, as if in a library. "You like?" she asks, swinging the braids around. They float up like Medusa's snakes.

"Yeah," I say. I'm not sure that I do, though. Her eyes look too naked somehow, too vulnerable. Sea green, almost luminescent. And I can hear Miranda in the back of my head. *Yeah. I think we need a little lesson here on cultural appropriation.* "Diego got them done for me."

"Ah," I say. I shift in the creaky office chair. "Don't you think he's kind of skeevy, though?" I'm hoping the question doesn't make her angry.

She doesn't seem put off. She tilts her head, considering it. "I dunno. Maybe." Then she shrugs, as if it's of little consequence. "He might be useful, though."

Before I can ask what that means, a man in a floral shirt shoots us a dirty look. We quiet down again, and the sound of keyboard tapping, with scattered coughs and yawns, fill the room. A barometer-clock ticks on the wall.

Jade's phone goes off, chiming with the sound of the cruise chat app, which we all downloaded the first day at the Hang Out. The app is basically texting, but just among other passengers on the ship. "It's Bryce," she says, putting the phone away without answering. "He's acting all pissy about me going off with Diego."

I debate whether to tell her, then figure I should, by the girl code. I would want to know if my boyfriend was talking shit about me. "He called you a bitch, you know," I say, making sure to whisper this time. "When you left with Diego."

"He did?" Her face registers hurt for a second, then she snuffs this out, her expression turning placid again. "Whatever. Won't be the first time. Won't be the last." She pulls her phone out again, probably to write something not very nice to him.

"Oh, hey," I say, risking floral shirt man's ire. "I wanted to show you something." Pulling out my phone, I get to the screen with Luke's text.

"Cool," she says, with a congratulatory smile. Then she

lets out a good-natured laugh. "Jelly Belly? What the hell is that?"

"Yeah, I know. Kinda dumb but—"

"No, it's cute," she says.

And while she's still distracted by it, I hit the forward button. Then I close my email, before anyone can see. "Ready to go?" I ask.

"Sure," she says, standing up from the desk. I stand up too, my body feeling light and trembly.

It's done. I've sent them.

No turning back now.

CHAPTER

eight

DAY 4

At Sea

The scent of coconut oil fills the air.

Yet another day at sea, where we can kill time until we get to Bermuda tomorrow. "Bermuda," my dad keeps saying with a sigh and a beatific smile, like the island is some earthly paradise, where everything joyous occurs. It probably is, but I'm just feeling mega-bitchy because I got my period. And still no word from Luke.

Lounging in a pool chair with my mom, I scratch my mosquito bites, which dot my body like constellations. I'm reading *The Great Gatsby*, which is a classic but so far seems like an overwritten book about self-absorbed white people. The ever-present steel drums with a conga line jerkily dancing around the pool isn't helping my concentration either. Trey splashes around with the other toddler Guppies in the kiddie pool across from us, his swimming diaper drooping.

Turning back to my book, I've read only one more paragraph when a shadow crawls over the page. My mom and I both look over to see the tall, looming figure of the captain. I have to lean my head back to see the whole length of him.

"Hello," he says in his booming Australian voice.

"Hi," I answer, trying to sound friendly since he is the captain after all, but failing to match his well-honed enthusiasm. My mom's *hi* sounds like mine.

"Enjoying yourselves, ladies?" he asks with a big fake smile. He smooths his rust-colored goatee with large freckled hands.

"Oh, yes," my mom answers. A seagull squawks overhead. "It's been just . . . lovely . . ." She turns to me.

"Oh, right." I clear my throat. "Yes. Very nice."

He gives us a confident nod. "Glad to hear it," he booms. The sun shines on his ginger-colored arm hair, bringing to mind a big red bear. "You let me know if you have any issues, okay?"

"Sure thing," my mom answers. Having satisfactorily executed his duty, he turns, briskly for such a large man. As he ventures on to the next customer on the pool deck, I hear the echo of his next greeting. *Enjoying yourself, fellas?*

"He seems nice," my mom says. My phone rattles on the plastic coffee table next to my mom's half-full piña colada, the whipped cream froth sunken in the heat. It's Miranda.

CALL ME.

"Is your data on?" my mom practically growls.

"No," I lie, trying to sound aggrieved that she would even think such a thing, and quickly switch it off. "Probably caught the Wi-Fi. It's just Miranda."

"Oh," she says, relief obvious in her voice. *Not that Luke, then.*

But I don't feel the same relief. She must have found out. Why else would she be trying so hard to get ahold of me? Dread washes over me. He said he wouldn't tell anyone if I helped him out. It was just this once, this one little thing.

But maybe he did tell people. And he hasn't even texted or emailed me back.

Trying to block out that thought, I turn back to my book. But after another few minutes reading about rich people complaining, I lift my eyes from the book and stare at the never-ending deep blue horizon. The conga line disperses, and the steel band plays Sam Cooke now. *Another Saturday night . . .*

"What would you think about getting a mani and pedi today?" my mom asks. "I'm getting a hot stone massage. I thought a little girl time might be fun. And you could look nice for the White Party tonight."

I assess my fingernails, chewed with ripped cuticles. It might be a good way to stop thinking about Luke at least.

"Jade could come too," she says.

———

A couple hours later, Jade and I sit side by side in huge sofa chairs at the spa, while New Agey music plays overhead. Jade's braids are out, her hair in kinky accordion curls. We await our pedicures while my mom is off getting her hot stone massage. The water lights up in blue, then green, then a lurid hot pink. Our chosen nail colors sit waiting on the trays—Firecracker Red for Jade, Margarita Lime for me. I notice that she has nubby pinkie toes, unlike my exceptional pinkie toes, one possible arena in which I outshine her.

"So why did you take out your braids?" I ask.

"Eh." She shrugs, twiddling her fingers. "Bryce didn't like them."

"Oh." That rubs me the wrong way. My mom has lectured me on all the red flags of abusive behavior as soon as I hit puberty. She's a divorce attorney for women, and said she's seen her share of abusive men.

Jade lets out a luxuriant yawn. "This was nice of your mom." She steals a look at her feet. "My mom would never have done that," she says, splashing the water with her toes. "Not in a million years."

My pedicurist, Dalisay, pulls my feet from the water and pats them off with a towel. Jade's pedicurist does the same. A squirting sound comes out of a bottle, and Dalisay rubs cold lotion up and down my legs. "And I'm thinking Joanie isn't into pedicures."

She hoots a laugh. "Yeah, right. She'd be happier if I fell off the ship." She adjusts the massager with the remote. "She'd probably push me herself, if it weren't for the money."

"What money?" I ask as Dalisay takes out a tray and picks up a tool.

Jade taps her fingers on the huge arm of the recliner. "My grandmother pretty much bribes them to take care of me." She forces out a laugh. "A bonus kicks in if they adopt me, I think."

Dalisay starts cutting my toenails, the clipper making a

sharp clacking noise with each squeeze. "That sounds fucked up," I say.

"It is fucked up," she agrees. The clacking sound continues, hers and mine. "And my uncle just spends it all anyway." Our pedicurists put those foam toe divider thingies on our feet, splaying out our toes. "Anyway, I'm working on getting me and my mom an apartment," she says, her tone more cheerful. "So she doesn't relapse this time."

Dalisay reaches for my color, then unscrews the top, a chemical scent filling the air.

"Where would you get the money for that?" I ask.

"I'm working some angles," she says with a shrug.

Her answer sounds purposefully vague, though, so I don't push her. Dalisay starts applying careful Margarita Lime strokes, the cold polish tickling my nails. Jade's pedicurist does the same, filling Jade's toenails with a bloodred color.

Our pedicurists finish up, and after the last coat dries, we take off, leaving my mom to her facial.

Awkwardly, we waddle back toward our room in our foam flip-flops on the hot deck. On the way, we pass by Diego. Jade pretends not to see him, but he calls out her name roughly. I wonder what changed since Coco Beach. . . . Trouble in paradise? She speeds up, so I follow. But hampered by our pedicures, Diego easily catches up. He throws his arm over Jade's shoulder, pulling her away from me. Maybe he means it to appear chummy, but it seems like he's gripping her arm.

"What?" she half whispers.

"I just want to talk," he hisses back.

Nerves swirling in my stomach, I take a step toward them.

"You want some help?" I ask in a normal volume. The tremble in my voice belies my toughness, though.

"I'm good," Jade says, rolling her eyes. "I'll text you about the White Party later?"

"Okay," I say, but still feel unnerved. I step away but stay close in case she needs me.

Diego herds her toward the railing, then takes his arm off her shoulder. She faces him, and he berates her in a low voice, knocking on the railing with a fist. She crosses her arms over her chest. I take a step toward her as he grabs her shirt, but then a passenger seems to take notice, and he releases it. Stumbling forward a step, Jade regains her footing and speeds away while he bellows after her.

"Jade!" he yells, but she keeps walking.

"You okay?" I ask, jogging to catch up with her. I'm short of breath with nerves.

"Yeah. He's just an asshole," she says, though she seems rattled.

A bang rings out, and we both look back as Diego pounds the railing again. Then he stomps off, his face a mask of fury.

CHAPTER
nine

After an excruciatingly long dinner with my family, in which my dad pored over every pamphlet for the perfect Bermudan excursion, and my mom decided we should discuss college applications (*We know Princeton is your top choice, honey, but just because your father went there doesn't mean you shouldn't look at other options*), I finally escape to Jade's room to prep for the White Party.

Jammed in her little bathroom, we share the mirror. I put on a seal-colored eyeliner, and Jade wears liquid black. She finishes with Taylor Swift–red lipstick, which I can't pull off, so I go with my usual shimmery lip gloss. After we deem ourselves presentable, we leave the cramped bathroom for her bedroom. Jade goes over to her nightstand and opens an expensive-looking forest-green necklace case with a snap. She unhooks a slim diamond choker and puts it on. You might think it would be overkill, but she makes it work.

"I love that," I say, pointing at it.

"Thanks," she says, fingering it.

"It's nice," I say. Even I know it's gauche to ask if it's real. But it looks real. Jade yanks open another drawer, and something slides on the wood. "You want to wear this?" She loops a silver pendant necklace with a sapphire jewel around her fingers.

"It's gorgeous," I say, tempted.

"Please," she says. "I want you to." Without allowing any objection, she moves behind me and does the clasp. Then she comes back around, smiling at her handiwork. "It looks really good on you." She shuts the drawer then. "It's from my mom."

"Oh," I say, starting to undo it in a flash. "I didn't realize."

"Don't be stupid," she says, then puts her hands up signaling no take backs. "I want you to wear it. And . . ." She smooths a wrinkle on her bed, looking down so I can't read her expression. "Keep it safe, okay? In case something should ever happen to me."

"What would happen to you?" I ask, catching her alarm.

She lets out a light laugh that seems forced. "Nothing. I'm being dramatic. Just . . . wear it for now."

"Okay," I say, touching the sapphire. "But I'm giving it back before the end of the trip." Right then, my phone buzzes with a text. I had dared to turn on the cellular for a bit, risking my mom's ire, and I'm rewarded with a message from Luke.

Hey, babe. Thanks a ton. You really saved my ass.

No problem, I write back.

"Is that Jelly Belly?" she asks, looping the strap of a little Kate Spade purse over her shoulder.

"Yeah," I admit, turning the cellular off while I remember. Looking down at the Crown Daily memo, I see *Rogue One* circled under Hang Out events. "You're planning on going to that?" I ask with a note of incredulity.

"Maybe," she says, pretending to be offended. "I love *Star Wars.*"

"Really?" I say, looking in the mirror to wipe off uneven lip gloss. "That doesn't seem like your type of thing."

"My mom likes all the *Star Wars* movies. She took me when I was little," she says, making wide eyes at the mirror. "I guess it must have rubbed off." She pauses then, as if thinking of something. "Wait a sec." She scribbles *J* on a key card, overlapping the *J* a few times to get the ink to stay on. "Keep this, in case we get separated."

I take the card with a shrug. "I could just knock."

"I just want you to have it," she says, trying to sound casual, but I hear anxiety in her words. "Just in case."

———

Jewel-colored strobe lights rotate over the white-clothed passengers, a disco ball throwing diamonds of light around us. We step into the dance area created by clearing out the tables and chairs from the Breakaway Café. The jostling crowd smells of shampoo and perfume, and a Dua Lipa song blasts on the speakers.

"Hey!" someone yells over the music. It's Caleb.

"Hey!" I yell back. Bryce stands next to him, drinking a soda. In the soft light, I can see the blondish hair stubbling his jaw. His white T-shirt hugs all his muscles. Maroon 5 comes on, and our quartet starts dancing. The DJ keeps the hits running, making stupid jokes between songs. Bryce turns out to be a surprisingly dorky dancer and Caleb a surprisingly smooth one. "Respect" comes on, and Jade lifts her arms, her choker dazzling in the lights. I don't know the next song, but we dance anyway, jumping to the thronging bass. I'm working up a sweat, hitting a natural high, when the music fades.

A slow song comes on then, John Legend's piano tinkling out. Most of the younger crowd vacates the floor as older couples start canoodling. In the distance, I see my mom and dad swaying, laughing together, which makes me feel weird, as if I'm spying on something private. Jade's aunt and uncle cling to each other as if he's just come back from a war.

Jade and Bryce move closer, about to dance, while Caleb looks wistfully at them, then turns to me. "You want to dance?" he asks.

My mouth actually opens in shock, but I catch myself and shut it. "Sure," I say, and we move closer. As fluid and entwined as Jade and Bryce are, we remain stiff and separate. His dry hand squeezes mine as we make it through the dance, then smile at each other with a mixture of relief and discomfort when it's done. As the song fades to scattered clapping, a voice comes over the intercom.

"Hello, everybody!" It's Leisha. "I'm looking for the Hang Out crew. Join me on the lido deck for a wild game of . . . Twister!" She yells the word so loud that feedback screeches in the microphone.

"Ooh, I love Twister," Caleb says. Again, without a whiff of irony.

Jade crosses her arms with a mysterious smile. "I have something *way* better than that."

CHAPTER

ten

Twinkling lights hang over the quiet, empty area by the pool, shimmering against the water and lending the space a romantic, Bohemian vibe.

We watch in silence as Jade pulls something out of her purse. It's a little plastic bag with black numbers marked on it and four white pills. "I got one for each of us," she says.

Caleb clears his throat. "Is that . . . like . . . aspirin or something?" he asks hopefully.

"Not exactly," she answers with a hint of a grin. "More like vitamins."

The DJ announces another song at the party. "Anyone here a Beatles fan?"

"Vitamins?" Caleb asks, squinting in confusion.

"Vitamin K, to be exact," she says, giving the bag a little shake.

"Oh, no," Bryce says, backing away a step, the realization dawning on him. He raises his voice. "I'm not doing fucking ketamine."

"Shh," Jade hisses. "Chill, Bryce."

"No, fucking way. We get tested for that shit," Bryce says,

but whispering now. "And I'm looking to go D2 next year, so no. Not happening."

She glances at me and Caleb as the dance floor sings "Let It Be" off-key. "I'm okay," I say in a reedy, pathetic little voice.

"Yeah, I'm good too," Caleb says. Though I wonder if he might have if Bryce had.

"Where did you get that shit anyway?" Bryce asks, stepping toward her again. He crosses his arms, his biceps bulging.

"Nowhere," she answers airily.

"Yeah, right," he says, shaking his head with a snort-laugh, and starts to walk away.

"Bryce," she calls after his back, sounding both sorry and annoyed. He lifts a dismissive hand and walks on. Needless to say, Caleb follows. "It was just an idea," she says quietly.

I play with the sapphire pendant, unsure of what to say, when we see a large figure emerging from the dance floor and striding toward us. As the person gets closer, the light reveals him to be the captain. At first, I think he's dressed in all white for the party, but then remember he's always dressed in white. "Ladies," he says in that Australian accent. "Enjoying the party, are we?" He says it like *pah-tee*.

"Sure," we both murmur. I notice her tuck the pills into her bag.

"We're not getting into any trouble out here?" he chides with a patronizing smile.

"Nope," I say. "No trouble." *I mean, what's a little ketamine between friends.*

"I'm just teasing," he says. "I know you're good girls." He

waits an awkward pause for us to verify this, and neither of us do.

"Ah, well," he says, "back to the party. No rest for the wicked, right? You girls stay out of trouble, okay?" We answer with weak *okay*s, then he walks back to the dance area, his shoes clomping smartly on the deck.

In the echo of his footsteps, I wonder if he is just being his usual glad-handing self.

Or if someone told him what Jade was up to.

———

We lie out on the loungers, as if we're suntanning by the moon.

But then Jade seems restless and gets up to sit on the edge of the pool. She leans over to brush the water, which ripples under her hand. A soft light bathes the pool area, the hot tub burbling nearby.

"Do you ever wish you could stay on a cruise forever?" she asks.

My immediate answer would be *hell no*. But something about her troubled expression makes me hold back. "I don't know. I've never really thought about it."

She takes her hand out, shaking the water off. "What's the worst thing you've ever done?"

"Okay, that's out of nowhere," I say with a chuckle, trying to deflect the question.

"What is it?" she asks, not appearing dissuaded. "The worst thing you've ever done?"

I swallow, glad she can't see me well in the shade.

I could tell her right now. I could tell her the truth. I cheated. I took pictures of the biology test and sent him my answers. I'll probably get suspended and never get into college and he's barely even acknowledged me. *You really saved my ass, babe.*

"I stole some lipstick," I say with no idea where that came from. Probably from being a total coward.

"Really?" she asks with surprise. "I've done that before. But I figured you were too good for that."

You obviously don't know me very well, I think. "What about you?" I ask, to take the spotlight off me. "What's the worst thing you've ever done?"

She doesn't speak right away, trailing her hand through the pool water. "I did something terrible to my mom." Her fingers make a figure eight in the blue water. Hypnotically, she moves her hand. "And she'll never forgive me for it."

I don't know what to say to this. "I'm sorry," I offer, feeling guilty at my lie, when she was so open with me. "But I'm sure whatever it was, wasn't your fault." A shriek of laughter sounds out from the dance floor, where they appear to be doing the limbo. *Jack be nimble, Jack be quick . . . underneath the limbo stick.*

"I was just trying to help us, though," she says, as if trying to convince me, or maybe herself. "I saved up a bunch of money. But then I was stupid enough to tell her where I kept it." Her face appears to slacken at the memory. "So we got kicked out of our apartment. And the judge sent me . . . with them."

I stick my hands through the plastic slats of the lounger, which squeeze my palms. "Because she didn't have enough money to take care of you?" I ask.

"Not exactly," she says, tracing the pool water again, maybe afraid to face me. "She used the money to get high, and I found her and . . ." She pauses, slapping the water now. "Well, someone found out," she says. "And she was declared . . . unfit or whatever."

A cheer sounds from the dance area, where the limbo appears to have ended.

"It's not your fault," I say again, which is useless, but I can't think of anything else.

"Yeah, I suppose," Jade says. She tosses off her sandals. "Okay," she says, injecting cheer into her voice. "Pity party's over. Who's ready for a swim?"

"Huh?" I ask.

She answers me by plunging into the pool. "Come on in," she says, shaking her slicked-back hair.

"But we're all dressed," I say.

"Eh," she says. With her body submerged except for her head, she looks like a mermaid. Her legs pivot gracefully. "You can wash your clothes later," she urges me.

They need a wash anyway. So I kick off my flip-flops. "What the hell," I say, and leap in, the water surprisingly warm. Air balloons under my dress as I sink. Jade kicks away from the wall in a practiced manner, as if she's done this move a thousand times, which she probably has. She swims across the pool, her arms arcing gracefully, her red-painted toes flashing with every kick. She seems to be floating on top of the water. Lap after lap she swims, her face occasionally twisting for air.

And I think about the sirens from the *Odyssey*, like Caleb talked about. And how maybe they were real. Gliding in the water, I stare up at the canopy of stars and wish I could bottle this moment, so I could come back to it whenever I needed to. When people are mean and life sucks and every other shitty thing happens. I could always come back to this lightness. Ketamine can't be any better than this.

As Jade comes near the edge again, her phone beeps. She pulls herself up by her arms, looking at the screen. Her white dress clings to her body. Then she comes back down into the water, catching her breath. "It's Bryce," she says. "He said he's sorry."

The phone beeps again, and this time she picks up the phone, careful to hold it on the sides. "He wants to meet up."

"Hmph," I say. Shocking. He's so, so sorry and coincidentally wants a booty call. So the bottled moment is officially over.

She types something into the chat, and a response flashes back. "We're meeting in my room," she says, and puts the phone back on the ledge. "Do you want to come?" she asks, though her tone asks me to decline.

"Nah," I say, and relief flashes across her face. "You go. Have fun."

CHAPTER

eleven

DAY 5

Arrival in Bermuda

After much debate and hand-wringing, my parents decide on the whale-watching Bermuda excursion. Thus, we motored around in the morning sun, while they tried to sell us drinks, until everyone was hot and cranky. And of course, no whales appeared for our viewing pleasure. There was some general grumbling about this, but also an asterisked statement in small print stating that actual results may vary and previous results do not guarantee future outcomes. Ergo, we may or may not see a whale. Trey manages to fall asleep on my lap and ends up peeing on my leg. So really, a swell time is had by all.

With my hair windblown, but not in a sexy way, and smelling strongly of urine, I board the ship again. My parents both look like they've been shot through a wind tunnel, and Trey is sucking his thumb, which he hasn't done in six months. The excursion was so bad, he is actually regressing.

Walking toward the pool, I see Bryce and Caleb lying on recliners. Caleb chirps away at him while Bryce grunts and stares at his phone. I sidle up next to them. "Hey."

"Hey," they both answer in unison. Bryce visors his eyes with his hand to see me.

"You guys doing any excursions?" I ask. I glance over at Caleb's tablet, which shows a game of chess midplay.

"Nah," Bryce says. "Just hanging."

He looks pretty tired, which is no surprise. Who knows how late they were up last night.

Caleb scrunches his noise, making a sniffing noise. "Something smells funny," he says.

Bryce takes an investigative sniff as well. "Yeah, like pee or something."

I take a step back. "Anyway, I gotta go. I'll see you guys later?"

"Yeah, we got volleyball at two, then the *Mortal Kombat* contest," Caleb announces.

"Right," I answer, and run off to shower before anyone else notices my urine perfume. As I'm bounding down the pool deck, my phone goes off in my hand. Then I remember I have the cell on since we're at port with Bermuda cell service. The text is from Miranda.

Are you ok?

He must have told. He probably showed his lacrosse bros the test during their tournament, and word spread. Jesus Christ I am so stupid.

About what? I ask, to see how much she knows.

Dots hang on the screen for a while, and my stomach

74

clenches. If she knows, everybody knows. My parents will kill me.

You didn't see it, then?

I'm sweating in the heat, my urine-stained shorts sticking to my legs. A kid yells *Cannonball!* and his shout is followed by a massive splash in the pool. Droplets thunk on the deck, landing on me like a smattering of raindrops.

See what? I respond.

The dots again. I wipe off the wet drops from the pool with a shaky hand.

Check Insta.

"Check Insta?" I say out loud. A server walks by with a tray of hamburgers and fries, the scent tantalizing, reminding me that I missed breakfast. Walking again, I tap the Instagram icon and see right away that Luke has a story up. So I click on it.

I let out a gasp, stopping in my tracks. My cheeks feel scalded.

Everything fades away. The caw of a seagull swooping overhead, the briny smell of salt mixed with lunch, the high-pitched, shrieking laughter by the pool. It all disappears. The only thing I can see is Luke, in bright Instagram colors, entwined with another girl.

Haley Pierce, a total bitch from my class who Luke supposedly hated, sits on his lap, her arms looped around his neck. In the end, it must have been more of a love-hate thing because she's practically giving him a lap dance, and they're kissing with animated hearts popping all around them. *This girl is so hot. #myjellybelly #drunk #springbreak*

I feel like I've been physically punched.

#myjellybelly. Jelly Belly. Of course. Jelly Belly wasn't a pet name for me at all. He wasn't even writing to me. He just sent it by mistake.

I turn away from the screen, and the outside scene rushes back in, the burning tops of my feet in flip-flops, the scent of diesel oil and dead fish, the never-ending screeching by the poolside.

In a daze, I start walking again, the phone sweating in my hand.

I just saw it, I type to Miranda, stabbing the keypad.

He's an asshole. . . . He doesn't deserve you.

With that, I turn off the phone. I don't have the energy for this discussion. *There are lots of fish in the sea. You have to kiss a lot of frogs to get to a prince. He's not worth it.* Blah. Blah. Blah. It's even more than that. I cheated for him. I risked everything, in the back of the classroom, my heart throbbing, snapping pictures of the exam with my phone as quick as I could when the teacher left for the bathroom. I cheated for him, and then he cheated on me.

I can't believe I'm such an idiot.

I get to my stateroom, without even remembering walking down the hall. Opening the door, I thank God that it's empty. I don't have to worry about putting on a happy face for everyone. I sit on my cot, putting the phone down. I knew he would dump me eventually, but not like this.

Lying down on my cot, I pull a blanket over my sweaty, pee-soaked body. I don't even care right now. I'm too exhausted to shower or do anything else. I wipe my tears away.

I'm not going to cry over that jerk. Miranda is right—he doesn't deserve me.

And now I'm going to get expelled for him.

I'll never get into Princeton, or any college.

I can't believe that I fell for it. I lay my head down, fighting tears, but after a while, I can't help it. My breath stutters, and my throat tightens. Tears creep out of the corners of my eyes.

So I snuggle my head into the pillow and just let myself cry.

CHAPTER

twelve

I feel about an inch better after a nap and a shower. Jade isn't answering her text-chats, so I check the Hang Out schedule and head to the Sports Deck in case she's there.

I find Caleb and Bryce on the basketball court next to the miniature golf, but no Jade. Caleb is dribbling a basketball, then takes a shot, his tongue dangling out. The ball misses, and Bryce grabs it and dunks it, then passes it back to Caleb, who throws another brick.

When Caleb sees me, he stops dribbling, looking happy for the excuse to stop playing.

"Hi," he says, holding the ball to the side on his hip. Then he steps closer to me. "Nice necklace," he says.

"Oh," I say, reaching up to touch it. It's Jade's sapphire pendant. I forgot I still had it on. "Thanks. Jade let me borrow it."

"Have you seen her by the way?" Bryce asks, bending down to tie his butterscotch-yellow Air Jordans. He glances up. "I went to her room, but she's not answering."

"I was going to ask you that," I say. "She isn't answering her phone either."

"She's probably still in a pissy mood," he says.

"Why, what happened?" I ask. "She was fine when I left her last night."

"I don't know," he says, sounding a touch defensive. "Something must have changed, I guess." He ties his other shoe. "She was acting all weird. Spacey."

"Maybe she's at the Hang Out," Caleb says, tossing the ball rapidly back and forth between his hands. "She could be in on the *Mortal Kombat* contest," he says hopefully.

"She wasn't there a little bit ago, but we could check," I say.

So we descend a few flights to the Hang Out. Two kids grip their video controllers, eyes laser focused on the screen, while a handful watch, but no blond heads among them. A menacing announcer voice says: "Round Two . . . Fight!"

"You guys wanna play?" Leisha asks.

The crowd of kids smells like a mix of sweat and body spray. "Nah," I say. "I think I'll sit this one out."

"Yeah, me too," Bryce says, appearing suddenly morose without his girlfriend.

"Yeah, I guess we don't need to play," Caleb says, though he looks like his pet just died. We leave the room, and I check my phone again, in case she left a message, but see nothing. We get to the hallway, and Bryce pushes the button to the elevator.

"Hey, if you see her, tell her I'm looking for her," Bryce says, tapping his foot.

"Will do," I say, deciding to take the stairs.

"Oh," he adds. "And tell her I'm sorry."

Then he steps onto the elevator. And I wonder what he has to be sorry for.

———

Later, I'm on the pool deck, baking in the sun and reading about conceited Daisy and her crew, trying to take my mind off Luke. It isn't working. After a few more pages, I start dozing off when a shadow crossing over my eyes wakes me up. I open them to see my dad towering over me.

He brushes his hand through his salt-and-pepper hair, which needs a cut. "Mind if I join you?" he asks, motioning to the empty recliner.

"Okay," I say, checking his expression. Is it a hey-let's-have-some-father-daughter-time look? Or is it an I-found-out-that-you-cheated-and-we-need-to-talk-about-it look? He lets out a big sigh, and I grit my teeth in anticipation.

But then he says, "This is the life, huh," and opens his book, which flaps in the wind.

"Yup," I say with relief. So father-daughter time—I can handle that. I turn back to Gatsby.

My dad gazes at the sky, his John Grisham book on his lap. "Where's your friend?" he asks.

"Dunno," I say. He smears lotion all over his hairy chest. Then he puts on his dorky huge earphones. With his polarized sunglasses, he vaguely resembles a hairy bug.

I try to concentrate again, but "YMCA" has started blasting out of the poolside speakers. Everyone in and out of the pool is jumping around and joining in. Of course, it reminds me of Luke again, dancing to this song at the Valentine's Day dance. He held my hips while I did the *Y,* kissing my neck. I turn back to my book and have gotten through literally one more paragraph when another shadow approaches. It's my mom, mouthing the words and making her arms into a *C.* Her hair looks like it's been teased in a million different directions. "That was an amazing yoga session," she says, throwing her beach bag on my dad's chair. She leans her arm on the top of my lounger. "Where's your friend?" she asks, looking around the area as if Jade might be hiding somewhere.

I let out an annoyed sigh. "I don't know. We're not conjoined, you know."

She drags a chair over, which clatters against the floor. "Well, excuse me for living," she says, plopping herself down.

"How was the yoga?" my dad bellows, above his noise-canceling headphones.

"A-ma-zing!"she yells back.

"Did you figure out if you wanted to do one of the specialty restaurants tonight? I was thinking Trey might like the hibachi table."

"Good idea!" my mom yells with a thumbs-up.

"YMCA . . . YMCA . . ."

I pop up from my seat. I'm not going to be able to read this book, even if I wanted to. And it wasn't helping me not think about Luke anyway. "Bye," I grumble, and grab my stuff.

Walking away, I hear my dad scream "What's wrong with her?" And my mom screams back "Hormones."

Just when I thought they couldn't be any more embarrassing, they find a way.

The sharp knife blade spins closer and closer to me, and then the chef tosses it into the air and catches it by the handle. The whole table claps appreciatively. My dad got us last-minute seats to the sold-out Hibachi Heaven and strutted around the stateroom like he scored us *Hamilton* tickets.

"*Choo-choo-choo-choo* . . . ," Haruto the chef says, then makes the steam rise from an onion pyramid.

"Wow," Trey says, his mouth wide open.

"Do you mind?" my mom asks, reaching for my soda. "Another headache."

"Be my guest," I say, pushing it over to her.

"Thanks," she says, and takes a big drink. "The caffeine really does help."

"You've been getting a lot of those, hon," my dad comments, while the chef catches an egg in his chef's hat, then splits it on his knife. The egg yolk sizzles on the table.

"It's just all the sun," my mom says, pushing my drink back, with a sizable amount missing now.

"Get ready for the fire," the chef exclaims, then pours a line of oil and lights it up. The fire explodes, and heat wafts onto my face. Trey's awestruck face is lit up orange.

My mom steals another sip of my drink, and my foot starts tapping. I'm getting a little worried about Jade now, though I shouldn't be. Maybe she got really drunk and is still sleeping it off. Or maybe she got pissed off with Bryce and is hanging out with Diego. Though I didn't see her when I passed by the casino and stole a look. On the other side of the table, a family is chanting "Sake, sake, sake!" while the chef squeezes a stream of sake into the father's mouth. My foot starts tapping again.

"You all right?" my mom asks, turning away from the sake family. "You seem off or something."

"I'm fine," I say, fidgeting with my fork.

"Is it about Luke?" she guesses as Haruto offers another family the sake treatment.

"No," I mutter. Yes.

"Is it about Jade?" she guesses next. "Did you guys get in a tiff or something?"

"No. We didn't get in a tiff." I enunciate *tiff*, to let her know it's the stupidest word ever.

"Here comes the snow." The chef tosses sesame seeds into the air, a strobe light making them look like snow.

"Snow," Trey repeats in wonder, following Haruto's every move.

"Oh, are you"—my mom lowers her voice—"on your menstrual cycle, honey?"

"God, Mom," I hiss. "Why don't you announce it to the whole table?" Abruptly, I stand up. "I'm going back to the room."

"Okay," my mom says. "We'll bring yours to go, okay?"

I don't answer, marching out of there as quickly as possible before my mom starts explaining the concept of uterine lining to the whole restaurant.

On the way to our room, I decide to check out Jade's room again. I know I'm overreacting, but it does seem weird not to make contact all day. Maybe she did end up taking the ketamine and got really sick from it. I would think her aunt and uncle would have checked on her, though. Outside her door, I knock loudly. "Jade?"

I'm about to walk away, when I think I hear something and put my ear flush up against the wood, straining to hear. I catch the faint rattle of cutlery and murmurs of conversation, but then realize the sounds emanate from the room next to hers. I try one more very loud knock and again wait in silence. No one answers.

Rifling through my purse, I find a pen but no paper. So I grab an empty gum wrapper, using the paper side of the peppermint-smelling tinfoil. I write against the wall, the ink streaky and faltering on the waxy underside.

What's up? Call me.

Izzy

Bending down, I shove it underneath her door, then head back to our cell of a room.

CHAPTER

thirteen

DAY 6

At Sea

After we leave Bermuda, Jade still hasn't appeared.

I'm both annoyed and concerned at this point. She's more than free to hang out with Bryce or Diego or whoever, but she could be polite enough to answer a text. Especially after I took the time to put a freaking note under her door.

Stopping by the Breakaway Café lunch buffet for an apple, I spy Bob and Joanie eating hamburgers. "Hi," I say, cleaning my apple with my shirt. Maybe they can give me an answer.

They both look up in surprise at the interruption. "Hi," Bob says, and Joanie nods a hello with her mouth full. His phone screen shows a TNC banking app, with different checking accounts, which seems just plain stupid. Even I know not to do banking over Wi-Fi with a thousand of your closest friends.

"Have you guys seen Jade lately?" I ask. Tossing the apple from one hand to the other, I do my best to look nonchalant and not stalker-y. "I haven't seen her since the White Party. And I knocked on her door and everything."

"Oh," Bob says, turning pink. He smooths his mustache, which has bread crumbs embedded in it, then glances briefly at his wife. "She wasn't feeling so great."

I grip the smooth, waxy apple. "Really?" I ask.

Bryce said she seemed spacey, but didn't mention her being sick. Although she could be overplaying a hangover, I suppose.

Bob clears his throat. "A flu, I think. She had a little fever, right, Joanie?"

"Yes," she answers, nodding fervently. "A fever."

"Really?" I ask again. It doesn't make a lot of sense, since neither a hangover nor ketamine would give her a fever.

Bob toys with a French fry, dunking it in ketchup. "Yeah, unfortunately. So she's holed up in the room. The staff suggested that. To keep her from infecting everyone else. She had . . . you know . . . diarrhea." He whispers the word, rendering it even grosser.

"Oh," I say, chiding myself. Here I am annoyed at her, and the poor girl is stuck in that cave-room with the runs, probably seasick on top of it. No wonder she didn't answer her door.

Though it was *really* quiet in there.

"Maybe I should visit her again," I say, half to myself.

Bob nearly chokes on his French fry. His face turns red, and he starts coughing. "I wouldn't," he says in his gravelly voice, pounding his chest. "She's probably sleeping."

"Yes," Joanie says, nodding with a saccharine smile. "I would let her get some rest, honey."

"Yeah, maybe," I say, taking a bite of the apple while Bob catches his breath again. I did leave her a note. That should be enough for now.

Explosions from *Rogue One* blast through the speakers.

Jade doesn't show. And considering she actually circled the movie on the sheet, she must be pretty sick. When I point this out to Bryce, he doesn't seem impressed.

"She's probably got a hangover," he says, staring impassively at the screen. His large hand dwarfs the carton of popcorn.

"Oh, this part's really cool," Caleb says, his hand disappearing into the popcorn box.

"Her aunt and uncle said she's really sick," I loud-whisper to Bryce, while Caleb makes blowing-up noises along with the screen. "She isn't even answering her door."

"She's probably with that asshole Diego," he says, his tone gruff. He doesn't sound overly concerned in any case. "I wouldn't go crazy over it. She's disappeared before. And last time—"

"Hey, did you guys hear?" Caleb asks, interrupting Bryce. He turns to look at us. "Supposedly the curse struck again."

"The curse?" My stomach shimmies.

"Yeah," Caleb says, shaking his popcorn box. "I was getting a snack after lunch." He glances around to make sure no one is listening. "And I overheard some people in the kitchen talking about it. Apparently somebody jumped."

Bryce eyes him, measuring whether or not to believe him. "Bullshit," he says finally, though doubt lingers in his voice. "They would have said something if that happened."

"That's the thing," Caleb whispers, laying his hands on his knees. "They said that they're covering it up."

The blood drains from my face.

"It isn't her, Izzy." Bryce gives me a sideways glance. "Yo, quit scaring everyone," he grumbles to Caleb.

"What?" Caleb asks, grabbing another handful of popcorn. "I'm just saying what I heard. I'm not saying it's Jade. Of course it isn't Jade."

As I stand up from the sofa, the ship lurches.

"Whoa," Caleb says, holding on to a cushion. "That must have been a *massive* wave."

"I have to go," I say, staggering as the ship tilts again.

———

"Jade," I say, fiercely whispering into the closed crack of the door.

Again, she doesn't answer.

I knock softly at first, which grows louder with every knock until I'm pounding.

"Jade!" I yell this time, and wait.

When she doesn't answer, I search for her *J* key card in my purse. But I must have put it in my other bag. So I take my own key card out of my purse to try it. The key slot buzzes but shines resolutely red. I try to jimmy the card through the crack in the door like they do on spy shows. But I'm not on a spy show and have no idea what I'm doing, so only manage to bend the card a smidge. I'm about to try to shoulder down the door, like they do on cop shows, when I see someone from the cleaning staff exiting a nearby room. The room next to Jade's has the DO NOT DISTURB sign on the knob, so he moves down toward me.

"Hi," I say, and he looks up at me with a smile. "I'm so sorry. I forgot my key."

He keeps smiling, but with a blank expression.

"Key," I say. I mime pushing a card in and then tapping my temple while shaking my head. The man just stares at me as if I'm crazy and, okay, so I'm not good at charades. I point to myself, then to the room, then throw my hands up.

"Oh," he says, with a nod of understanding. "Yes." He fumbles around in his pocket and pulls out a key card punched through with a blue plastic coil. As he slips it through the key slot, the light turns green, and I put my hands in prayer as a thank-you. He smiles and glances in. "Clean?" he asks.

"No," I say. "It's good. Thank you." I casually move inside as he pushes his cart to the next room, the wheels squeaking and rattling.

The first thing I notice is my little gum-wrapper note still on the floor. Then I look up to see the bed tightly made, with no sick Jade in it. "Jade!" I yell, yanking the bathroom door open to nicely organized toiletries, the towels symmetrically hung, the toothbrush sitting in a glass. I touch the bristles, which are bone-dry.

"Jade?" I call out again, hearing the desperation in my

voice. And then I notice her pillow with two chocolates on it, untouched.

Two chocolates. Two nights.

"Jade!" I yell, holding back tears.

But she doesn't answer. Because she isn't here.

She's gone.

CHAPTER

fourteen

"She must be somewhere on the ship," my dad says when I race back to our room to tell him. He fits Trey's limp, sleepy body into his sleeper pj's. The footies take a couple of yanks.

"She hasn't been there in two days now, Dad," I insist. "And her toothbrush was dry."

My mom shrugs. "Maybe she just doesn't brush her teeth."

"Of course she brushes her teeth," I yelp, and my mom does a shushing motion and points to Trey. My dad arranges him in the crib as he mewls and tosses his head to the side, his cheeks rosy and his little fish-mouth open.

"This is important," I plead, tears pricking my eyes. "How come nobody believes me?"

My mom's face fills with pity. "Of course we believe you, honey. It's just . . ." She plops down on the bed. "Maybe you're overreacting. People don't just go missing on cruise ships."

But they do, according to Caleb. They would never believe that either, though. I bite my hangnail in agitation.

"Okay," my mom says, her face straightening, all business. "Where did you see her last?"

"Mom," I snap. "It's not like I lost my phone. I didn't leave her anywhere. She hasn't been in her room for two days. And her aunt and uncle are totally lying about it."

My dad raises his eyebrows, looking dubious. "Now, that's a pretty serious accusation to throw around."

"And it's pretty serious that she hasn't been in her room in two days," I shoot back, chewing my finger again.

"I'm just saying let's not make a mountain out of a mole-hill here," my dad says in that calm-down tone, which usually sends my mom into conniptions. I can see where she's coming from now.

"Why don't you check the Hang Out?" my mom asks, a yawn escaping her mouth.

"I did," I say. "Like a hundred times."

"Or maybe ask that boy she likes?" she suggests. "The handsome one?"

"I did," I repeat, louder this time, and they both simultaneously shush me and point to Trey. So I march out of the room, before I start screaming bloody murder at them both.

———

"I'm sure it's nothing," Leisha says when I explain the situation to her. She's closing up the Hang Out after the movie. "But I agree, we need to make sure she's okay. So let me call Toni, our cruise director."

I let out a breath of relief. Finally, someone who will listen to me.

She grabs her walkie-talkie off her desk. "This is Leisha Evans, over." Her voice transforms from babysitter-esque to impressively official. A squawked response comes back. "We have a potential missing passenger here. Reported by her friend as missing now for"—she turns to me, and I put up two fingers—"two days."

"Copy that . . ." a woman on the other end answers with a snappy British accent. "Letting"—*static, static*—"First Lieutenant Johnson"—*static, static*—"will let you know the plan"—*static, static*

"Copy that," Leisha answers, then puts the handheld back down on the desk.

"And her toothbrush was dry," I say. "Did I tell you her toothbrush was dry?"

"Yes, you did," she answers, back to her patronizing babysitter tone. "But that just means she didn't sleep in her room. It doesn't mean she didn't sleep somewhere else."

I bite my lip, horrified at the thought. "So you think someone could be hiding her?" My voice rises an octave. "That they kidnapped her?"

"No," she says slowly, in the same calm-down tone that my dad had. "I didn't say that. What I'm saying is that she might be staying somewhere else on her own accord. As in, voluntarily." The handheld device pops with static on the desk, as if coming alive. "Toni here"—*static, static*—"over."

Leisha pushes the button. "Over."

"All right, then," Toni says over the walkie-talkie, the sound fading in and out. "We're going to"—*static, static*—"missing person drill first. Then if that's negative"—*static, static*—"skipper's"—*static, static*—"call a muster."

"Copy," Leisha says. "Over." Then she turns to me. "Hang tight, okay? We'll find Jade. Don't you worry."

I don't hear anything more and decide to go back to the room and get some sleep.

On the way back, the Bon Voyage Theater lets out the late show, a country-western revue that my parents decided to skip. In the midst of the crowd, Joanie emerges without Bob, which seems weird. She smiles, chatting with the woman behind her, not seeming worried in the least. I'm not sure if this makes me feel better or not. If she's not concerned, then maybe I shouldn't be. But then, if she and Bob are lying to me, maybe I should be.

Fighting through the throng, I make my way to her. "Hi," I say, practically yelling above the din of the exiting audience. I could swear that Joanie sees me but swerves in the opposite direction. "Hey, Mrs. Gibson," I say again in a loud voice. But she just keeps walking, as if she didn't hear.

Is she hiding something?

Frustrated, I take the stairs to our deck. My parents have clicked off their lights already. My mom murmurs a sleepy good night to me, my dad already out cold. Trey remains silent in the crib.

I put on my pj's and lie down, but sleep doesn't come easily. I toss and turn in the creaky cot, staring at the dried drip of paint on the ceiling, the low moan of the ship's motor underneath me. When I close my eyes, I see Diego grabbing her arm, Bryce glaring at her, and Joanie moving away from me. I see Jade in the pool, her hair slicked back and shiny.

I don't remember falling asleep, but I must have because

two hours later, the captain's voice jolts me awake. "Good evening, passengers. This is your captain speaking." His booming voice sounds more reassuring than hearty this time. My parents jolt up in bed.

"I repeat, this is your captain speaking. I'm sorry to disturb you. But we are going to do a mandatory lifeboat drill." His voice echoes across the ship.

"A lifeboat drill?" my dad asks with incredulity, his voice husky with sleep. He consults his watch. "At two o'clock in the morning?"

But I know what this means immediately. It's like the cruise director told Leisha. The missing person drill must have been a bust, and now they're checking for all the passengers.

Jade isn't sick in her room. She isn't hanging out with Diego or having some secret romantic rendezvous.

She's gone.

"I repeat, this is your captain speaking," the voice drones. "We are going to do a mandatory drill."

Trey mumbles something in his sleep while my mom switches on the lamp, which stings my eyes. In the stark relief of the light, our windowless room looks cramped and messy. She throws on jeans under her nightshirt; my dad stays in his pajamas and puts on his flip-flops. I shove on some sweats and slip-ons.

"We ask that you calmly exit your rooms and follow your crew member's instructions. There is no reason for panic, but we do ask that every member of your party take part in this head count." The captain sounds like he's reading from a script.

"Wait," my mom says, her eyes narrowing. "Did he say *head count?*"

There is a pause, and she glances at my father, who gives her a worried look in response.

"Yes," I say numbly. "He said *head count.*"

Neither answers, but their silence tells me they both understand what this means. That I'm not some hysterical teenager full of drama. That my friend has disappeared. I feel no satisfaction in this victory. In fact, I feel like I might throw up.

My dad swoops Trey up from the crib, who immediately snuggles himself into a sleeping position on my dad's shoulder. My mom picks up Trey's blanket and puts on her huge purple glasses, and we follow the crew members to our lifeboat stations.

Moonlight bathes the decks, which are brimming with grumbling, sleepy passengers. Crew members roam around, polite but officious, doing a rapid head count.

I think back to the usual lifeboat drill on the first day of every cruise that I've taken. Passengers go through the motions but just want to get through with the formality already so they can "par-tay," hit the beach chairs, the shuffleboard, the bars. The atmosphere is nothing like that tonight, feeling somber and quiet, otherworldly. In each pod, the crew member checks our photo on their tablet and ticks our names off. Numbers are tabulated, spoken out loud. The ship crawls, slower than the usual velocity at night, the constant drone of the motor noticeably absent.

They aren't going to find her. They're never going to find

her. My chest tightens, and I take a breath. I shouldn't think the worst. Maybe this is where they find her. Maybe in the morning, this will all seem like a bad dream. But I know I'm lying to myself.

Finally, we are given the all clear, and the mass of grumbling passengers starts filtering back inside. In the hallway, my pod merges with Bryce's, and we walk together for a few paces. I clear my throat to say something, but he avoids my eyes.

I say his name, but he doesn't answer, disappearing into his group.

CHAPTER
fifteen

DAY 7
At Sea

After the drill, the ship reverses course back to Bermuda.

First thing in the morning, I run to the Hang Out, and thankfully, Leisha is there.

"Did they find anything?" I ask, short of breath from the jog over.

But the look on her face says it all. "I'm sorry, Izzy," she says with tenderness. "But don't give up hope. We're still looking for her."

"Uh-huh," I say, choking out the word with a nod. Then I get out of the room, before she can see me cry. I fight tears all the way back to our room. The ships feels different, the mood apprehensive instead of carefree. Overhead, Toni the cruise director announces a Jungle Day, her voice full of desperate cheer. I can see *The Jungle Book* already playing on the pool deck's flat-screen, and fake plastic greenery has been strewn everywhere.

I get back to the room, my eyes dry. But my mom takes

one look at me and goes into comforting-mom mode. I can't say that I really mind.

"Did Leisha say Jade was missing?" she asks.

I nod, trying not to cry. As I sit on the cot, she takes a seat next to me. "You want to hang out in the room today?" she asks. "I can stay with you."

Meanwhile, Trey remains oblivious, as a toddler should. He chases a beach ball around the room, grabs it, then slaps it away to chase again. Essentially playing a game of fetch with himself.

"Or maybe we could sit by the pool?" she asks. "You could read your book?"

I know she's just trying to be nice, but I'll go crazy sitting in the room, or even at the pool. And there's no way I can let *The Great Gatsby* into my headspace right now. "Think I'll walk around the ship a little bit."

"Okay," she says, but she looks worried.

"Nothing's going to happen to me," I say, standing up from the cot. Trey tosses the ball up high, where it whacks the ceiling and ricochets around the room, knocking over suntan lotions and water bottles.

"Trey," my mom scolds as he toddles after the ball again.

"I'm just going to the computer room," I say, tucking my key card in my purse.

"Okay," my mom says, biting her bottom lip. "And you can use more than ten minutes on the internet if you want. Since it's another day at sea."

And since not too much harm can befall me in a computer room. But at least she's giving me more time on the internet.

Before I can even leave, a loud noise arises from above us, a rhythmic *thack-thack-thack-thack.* . . . We all look up to the noise, as if we might be able to see it through the ceiling. "What's that?" I ask.

"I'm not sure," my mom says. The noise expands, the clacking faster, almost deafening. "I think it's a helicopter," she says, almost yelling to be heard.

"Helicopter?" Trey says, his eyes lit up with delight. "Like Harold?"

"Who's Harold?" I yell, befuddled.

"From Thomas," she yells back. "The train."

Trey delves into his toy bag to find it, the white wooden helicopter with a smiley face. Abandoning the fetch game, he buzzes the copter around the room.

"Maybe they found her!" I yell to my mom. "Maybe they're bringing her back." I pull out my phone. "I could ask Leisha."

My mom gives me a sad smile and puts her arm on my shoulder. "It might just be the police," she says, her voice almost drowned out by the noise.

And she's probably right. If the police are here, it means one thing.

They think Jade is dead.

———

The usual sedate atmosphere of the computer room has shifted to apprehensive, tension stretching the air. I catch snippets of multiple whispered conversations speculating about last night. *I heard someone committed suicide. It's so awful . . . right?*

I focus on the noise of the buzzing fluorescent and start by googling Jade's name. But nothing comes up. So the media hasn't caught on to it yet. Next I search "the curse of the *Crown Jewel*," and again, find nothing, just a ton of ads for the cruise ship coming up. I change the search to "death and cruise ships," which gets a fair number of hits, including an Agatha Christie book and one particularly juicy article called "Death on Cruise Ships: The Industry's Dirty Little Secret." Perusing the article, I find different ship lines mentioned, and more than a few anonymous sources, but nothing about the *Crown Jewel.*

I heard she was pushed . . . by her boyfriend.

Either Caleb is fibbing or the *Crown Jewel* has a top-notch PR team.

I move on to social media, hoping her networks will prove more fruitful.

Insta has mostly bikini selfies with people commenting *"you're so beautiful!" "wow, you look amazing," "wish I was there,"* and the like. And if I had her body, I'd take a million self-ies in a bikini too. She also took a selfie with Bryce, who looks as happy as I've ever seen him, with the sunset in the background. I didn't follow her on Snapchat, so I move on to TikTok. No need to bother with Facebook where she has a shadow account, since that's the only one Bob and Joanie know how to check, posting extremely benign crap about friendship and swim meets and not doing drugs.

My friend heard it was an accident. Some guy got really drunk and fell over the railing.

On her TikTok, there's a video of her boarding the ship,

the camera rocking enough to cause motion sickness. She took one of me, with a mock-serious voice-over saying, "Izzy is about to go to a magic show everyone." My face is flushed, and I start jumping up and down and screaming, "I CAN'T WAIT TO GO TO THE MAGIC SHOW!" The camera shakes as she laughs. I remember this video, when we were about two mini-bottles in. I didn't know she posted it, though. The next video shows her doing the dead man's float while Caleb gives a voice-over: "Oh no, folks . . . I think she's a goner. . . . Poor, poor Jade. We're all going to miss her smiles and her absolutely horrendous foosball skills, and . . ." Then she pops up with a huge grin, and he says, "Folks! It's a miracle! She lives!"

The video chills me. If this were a novel, I would think it was way too on the nose. But in any case, it's not at all helpful in finding her. Neither of these things would have anything to do with her disappearance. I'm about to finally log off when I see one more video on TikTok, taken the night she went missing. She's wearing her white dress, which has partially dried from the pool but still sticks to her, her necklace gleaming, sending dots of light careening into the camera. "Come on . . . ," she says, laughing so hard she's gasping for breath. "Just this once . . ." Her words sound slurred and off, though that could just be the laughter. "Pleeease . . . ," she says, and a shadow dashes across the lens.

"I said I didn't want to," a man complains in a low voice, and her laughter rings out in response. Someone yelling in the background obscures the voice.

"Fine, fine, grumpy," she jokes, and the video ends. I watch it again. Over and over.

But I can't figure out whose voice it is. And the only clue is a flash of white clothing before the hand blocks everything. Of course, either Diego or Bryce would be the obvious choice. But it doesn't really sound like either of them. I play the video one more time before a message pops up.

Oh no! Sorry to spoil your surfing . . . but it appears you've gone over your internet limit! Don't worry . . . you can still easily load up on more minutes at the gift shop, the front desk, or right here with your credit card!

But I don't have a credit card. I try to move the mouse, but the screen is frozen on the dumb passive-aggressive message. "Shit," I say, and a few heads turn toward me.

As I walk out, the low voice from TikTok keeps replaying in my mind, and I think of Bryce, gliding away from me at the head count.

Hey, you guys around? I chat Caleb, figuring Bryce can't be too far.

Hanging, he answers. *What's up?*

Can we meet up? Talk about Jade?

Okay, Caleb chats back. *Blue Velvet Lounge?*

The voice loops in my head. *I said I didn't want to. I said I didn't want to.*

It could be anyone.

It could be the last person to see her alive.

Be there in 10 minutes.

103

CHAPTER

sixteen

When I arrive at the Blue Velvet Lounge, a bouncy piano tune greets me.

Oh, when the saints . . . go marching in . . .

The music abruptly stops, leaving an oppressive silence. Then Caleb emerges from behind the shiny, black player piano. "Sorry," he says. "I was just killing time."

Bryce sits on a C-shaped couch, drinking soda from a straw. Caleb joins him, leaving me with a stiff seat that doubles as a coffee table. The lounge is really just a space between the casino and the dining room, dimly lit with jazzy piano playing by night, and dull and overdressed by day.

As I sit, the royal-blue velour smells of smoke and tickles the back of my legs. The sun streams down through a window, illuminating a triangle on the rug in front of me and blinding my eyes. "So," I say.

No one answers my opening. Caleb plays air piano while Bryce keeps sipping his drink.

I carry on. "Leisha said they're still looking for her. I was checking if you guys heard anything."

Bryce stares at his soda. "We would have told you if we did."

I try to read his expression, but it's blank. Not nervous or guilty, just sad, if anything. "Maybe we should look too," I say. "I was thinking if she took the ketamine, maybe she's hurt or something."

They both glance at me with disbelief, then Caleb sits on his hands, and Bryce takes a loud slurp of his soda.

"What?" I ask to their obvious discomfort. They don't appear guilty, so much as pitying. Like when my dog, Casper, died and my mom told me he went to the farm.

"You don't think she's alive?" I ask. "That it's at least possible?" Again, no one answers.

Finally, Bryce sighs, breaking the silence. "I think it's doubtful, Izzy," he says.

"Why?" I ask, squinting against the sun.

Bryce's knee starts bouncing. "I would love to believe that. Honestly, I would. But . . . think about it, Izzy. People don't just vanish into thin air. If she's not on the ship, she's in the water. Which means she's probably . . ." He takes another drink instead of saying the word.

"She could still be somewhere," I argue, "in hiding, maybe." Bryce plays with his straw, not looking at me. "Or in Bermuda. Leisha said they're still looking for her. No one is assuming she's . . ." I don't say the word either.

They stay silent. I bite my lip to ward off angry tears coming on. "You guys are friends with her too. Don't you care a teeny little bit about her?"

"Yes, we care, Izzy," Bryce snaps. "Don't be all high-and-mighty, like you were the only one who knew her." He throws his hands into the air. "I'm just not acting like an idiot. She's not on the fucking ship hiding somewhere. So no, I'm not going to join your little search party. She's obviously dead. And I don't know what you expect me to do about that."

Silence follows this diatribe as Caleb's hand rattles a bowl of peanuts. He eats them, the chewing sound noxious in the silence. The sun beats down on my scalp, and I shift on the seat to escape it again. I read Bryce's expression, but he just seems his usual annoyed self, and Caleb just seems uncomfortable with the situation.

"There's something I wanted to show you," I say, retrieving my phone where I saved the video. "It's Jade's TikTok."

I lay the phone on the table, and they both lean forward to see. The short clip plays, ending with her "fine, fine, grumpy" and laughing admonishment, then the flash of white, the squealing and splashing in the background, and the hand covering the lens.

"Play it again," Caleb says, moving even closer. So I do, and he leans closer. *I said I didn't want to.* He purses his lips, as if he might recognize the voice.

"What do you think?" I ask, putting my phone away. I check Bryce's expression, but he has no tells—no blushing, no nervous tics, no twiddling fingers. Nothing.

Bryce shrugs. "It's not me," he says. "I can tell you that much."

"Yeah," Caleb agrees, and takes a sip of his Coke. "It doesn't really sound like you."

And yet you feel the need to exonerate yourself, I think. "I wasn't saying that. I just wondered if you recognized the person."

"From that?" Bryce scoffs. His knee starts bouncing again. "Could be anyone."

"Diego?" I ask.

His face sours then, his fists tightening. So maybe this is his tell. "Probably," he says. "Or it might be her uncle. He has that kind of low voice."

This gives me pause. "Yeah, he does kind of have a similar voice."

But before I can think about it anymore, two men head toward us, their faces washed-out by the sun. As they get closer, they are revealed as Bermudian police officers. They look oddly casual in their powder blue shirts and black shorts with long black socks. One of the men looks nervous and young, like a newly minted cop. He's white with mousy brown hair and skinny calves. The other man wears a confident smile and appears like the higher-ranking officer. He's Black, with flecks of gray in his sideburns, and a fit build.

"Bryce Thompson?" he asks.

"Yeah," Bryce answers, his voice wavering between nervous and belligerent.

"Inspector Curtis," he says. His stony expression softens with his broad smile as he reaches his hand out to shake. He has an odd accent, sort of English, but not. "Do you mind coming with us for a moment?"

Bryce glances at us, as if we could save him, and we stare back helplessly. "Yeah, sure," he says, standing up, as they wait for him to gather his phone and room key. Then they walk away with him.

We sit in dead silence as they leave, and I release a breath. Maybe he has nothing to do with it. But maybe he does. Why did he feel the need to immediately deny that it was him on the video?

And I've seen him act controlling. I've heard him call her a bitch. And even more than that, I know he asked her to meet up with him that night. The truth is: He was the last to see her, and he can't quite meet my eyes when we talk about her. He knows something. He must.

"Do you think he's involved?" I ask, in a whisper.

But Caleb shoots me a look of disgust. "No," he says loudly. "Whatever happened to Jade, he's got nothing to do with it."

CHAPTER

seventeen

After Bryce leaves, Caleb does too.

Aimlessly, I wander around the ship, but nothing feels right. The whole ship appears staged somehow. As I walk by the pool, the steel drums once again playing "No Woman, No Cry" seem obscene, artificially constructed cheer for an audience of kids squealing in the pool and adults raiding the never-ending buffet like nothing ever happened. I want to scream at everyone on the pool deck. *Don't you get it? My friend is missing!* But everyone just keeps going along with their stupid cruise as if nothing ever happened. As if my friend didn't just disappear.

After leaving, I pass the 24-7 Caffeine Fix kiosk and consider getting a chai tea, my go-to comfort drink. I could use the caffeine, since my body feels weighed down, and my head feels cloudy and exhausted. It's probably from being up late last night. But the caffeine will just make me jumpy and upset. Passing the casino, I notice Sergei the bouncer sidling next to a man who looks drunk and is sobbing.

Across the way, a sign announces a matinee of *Casablanca* playing in the Bon Voyage Theater. I can hear murmurs from the movie, the sound effects of a car screeching. I open the door, letting light into the mostly empty room and a few annoyed patrons squint at me, then turn back to the screen as the door sweeps shut. For some reason, I think maybe she could be in there. It would be the perfect place to hide, sitting in the dark, camouflaged as any other member of the audience. So I jog quickly up and down the aisles, ignoring the dirty looks of the moviegoers. There aren't many of them, though, and Jade isn't one of them.

Dejected, I leave the theater. It was a stupid idea. Of course Jade isn't in there.

I keep walking, half killing time and half looking for her, staving off the painful reality that Bryce and Caleb are probably right. I'm just deluding myself with false hope. Still, I go down one more flight to check the *Crown Jewel*'s mall area.

The typical gift shop fare beckons—costly *Crown Jewel* hoodies, in case you want to pay for the honor of advertising their ship, and a kiosk of *Crown Jewel* magnets and can openers, magazines, and overpriced packs of crayons and paper, lining the wall (for desperate parents, I suppose). Then I swing across the hall to the more sedate, luxurious store. The brassy scent of cologne coats the air. I touch the soft cashmere of pashmina shawls in bright jewel tones, and check the endless bottles of duty-free liquor, followed by the endless bottles of duty-free perfume. Necklaces and bracelets lie atop plastic models in the glass case. Topaz rings and ladybug broaches with gaudy rubies. I even see what look like engagement rings (for desperate suitors, I suppose). I'm about to leave, since it's lunchtime anyway, when a necklace catches my eye.

Under the hot glass, a thin gold choker lined with diamonds shines, the exact one that Jade was wearing the night of the White Party. "How much is that one?" I ask, pointing to it.

The worker with severe eye shadow and gelled-up short hair eyes me with suspicion. She readjusts her leopard-print pashmina with long, maroon fingernails. "Probably more than you can afford," she says with a get-lost-kid smile.

"How do you know what I can afford?" I ask, trying my best to sound wealthy, pretentious, and snobby. Someone like Daisy Buchanan. (At least this book has been good for something.)

The woman reassesses me, perhaps gauging whether I might indeed be some spoiled rich kid and she could actually make a sale. Her smile widens a smidge. "Five thousand dollars," she says.

"Five *thousand*?" I yelp, losing every ounce of my cool.

Her smile thins again. "As I said, more than you can afford."

But not more than Jade could afford, apparently. Unless someone bought it for her. I take my hand off the hot glass, leaving the glaze of a sweaty handprint. "Do you know the last person who bought that?" I ask, trying to sound casual and curious.

She steps away from the counter. "I'm afraid I can't divulge that kind of information."

I'm trying to think of another approach when I remember the *J* card in my purse. Maybe I could do some digging on my own.

With a renewed hope, I race down the three flights to our deck. I stride down the hallway with my card in hand, trying to appear nonchalant and purposeful when I stop.

There's a guard sitting in a chair outside the room. He's got on the powder-blue shirt and Bermudas outfit, but I don't recognize him as one of the investigators. Wearing a severe expression, he has his arms crossed, and nods a hello at me. I nod back with a smile, marching past him.

Damn it.

———

I push my shrimp Alfredo around on the plate.

Tonight is cartoon night in the dining hall. SpongeBob made an appearance, which blew Trey's mind like a bad trip. He turned white and started sobbing, before being quickly calmed with peanut butter and jelly. But I'm not hungry at all. I can't help but glance over at Jade's usual table, where her aunt and uncle sit by the fake candlelight. Joanie eats her dish with a napkin tucked under the collar of her dress, but Bob keeps checking his phone. Not exactly romantic, perhaps, but they still don't appear overly bothered by Jade's absence.

"May I be excused?" I ask. Maybe on my way back to the room, I could quickly stop by their table again.

"Um, sure. You're not hungry?" Mom asks, worry weighing in her voice.

"Not really," I say as SpongeBob madly waves his arms in the corner across the room. "I was thinking I might just go back to the room."

"Do you have a migraine?" she asks, reaching into her

purse for her pill bottle. "You can take it with some caffeine. It helps."

"No," I say. "Just exhausted. I might get to bed early."

"Okay," she says, fretting. But then her face brightens. "Why don't you take Trey with you?"

"Take Trey with me?" I'm not sure which part of *I'm exhausted and want to go to bed* translates into *I want to supervise a toddler*, but she probably figures I can't get in too much trouble dragging my little brother along with me. But it also means I can't approach Bob and Joanie.

Trey starts bouncing on his booster seat in response. "ZiZi! ZiZi!" he squeals. "ZiZi!"

"Here, Trey," I say, figuring there's no getting around it now. He takes my hand, and we walk out of the dining room, moving around the long line of passengers snaking around the lobby. We wait by the elevator, and Trey starts bopping up and down like a popcorn kernel when it finally comes. Everyone in the elevator gives us an isn't-he-cute smile.

"I push," he says. "I push."

"Okay," I say. "Hit four." This assumes, idiotically, that Trey knows his numbers, which he does not. So he pushes the whole row of floors to a general groan in the elevator. The isn't-he-cute crowd has turned against us. "Sorry," I say, swooping him up before he can hit any more buttons. I ferry him off on our floor, leaving the passengers to slowly ride the rest of the way, and we head toward our room. I would love to rest in our room, but that won't be easy while attached to a rambunctious toddler.

Trey holds my hand, swinging it. "Upsy!" he yells.

"Not right now," I say. He means the upsy-daisy game, where I swing him up and down by the arms while saying *upsy-daisy*.

"Upsy!" he yells again. A command, not a request.

"I'm tired, Trey. Let's do it later." Then we pass by Jade's room.

And the chair sits there, empty.

I have a lightning-fast debate with myself. While I hate to drag Trey into this, we might not have another chance to get in her room. "How would you like to do something fun?"

"Okay . . . ," he says, like there might be a catch. Sometimes he is wise beyond his years.

"Let's go to another room and investigate," I say, drumming up excitement in my voice. He doesn't look convinced however. "Like . . . explorers," I say, since Dora the Explorer is his new favorite thing ever.

His eyes light up. "Find dinosaurs?" he asks.

"Maybe," I say. I highly doubt we'll find dinosaurs in Jade's room, but I need his cooperation right now. "Yes, let's find some dinosaurs."

———

I make a quick check around the area and see no one. So I pull the card with the *J* on it, praying they haven't changed the code. The key mount whirs and turns green.

"Where we go?" Trey inquires loudly.

"Shh," I say, opening the door and giving him a little push in.

"We look for dinosaurs?" he asks, checking in case I forgot.

"Yes," I whisper, and start poking around. I don't even know what I'm looking for truthfully. The room appears pretty much the same as when I last saw it. A few pamphlets have been moved, some drawers remain open, the rug with crosshatch marks from vacuuming.

"Go home," Trey complains, perhaps realizing I've pulled one over on him.

"One sec," I whisper. My eyes scan the room, and light upon the safe. I remember the code from before, October thirteenth, her mom's birthday, which also happens to be Miranda's birthday. It makes me wonder for a second if her mom even knows she's missing.

I key in 10-13, and the message blinks *open*. Peering inside, I expect to see nothing, or maybe her necklace. But a thick manilla envelope sits in the space. I slide it out, forgetting about fingerprints until I've already touched it. The envelope is unsealed, and I lift open the flap.

I let out a gasp.

"Dinosaur?" Trey asks, sounding skeptical that one could fit in there.

"Maybe in the bathroom," I advise, and he runs in to check, while I peer through the envelope. No dinosaurs. No necklace.

Just money, lots of it.

There's a mess of hundred-dollar bills in there. In shock, I thumb through the greasy, soft bills, counting them as fast as I can. It's probably about ten thousand dollars.

Where did she get all this money?

"Go," Trey demands, emerging from the dinosaur-less bathroom.

With no good plan, I stash the money back into the safe and lock it up again with the code. I glance around the room for any more clues, then remember it, that purple journal I saw in her backpack at the beach. But I find only two books, *The Fault in Our Stars,* which made me ugly cry, and *The Woman in Cabin 10,* which I never read. I start opening and shutting drawers to find the journal when I hear footsteps coming from down the hall. I hold my breath, and they come even closer.

My heart stills.

"Go," Trey repeats.

So I make a split-second decision. We could hide, but it would never work, especially with Trey. Best we can do is leave as quickly as we can and think of a cover story later. Maybe I'm just a nosy passenger and I swear the door wasn't completely shut. Maybe I was looking everywhere for my little brother and somehow he got in that room.

"Let's go," I whisper, and walk out as calmly as possible. We've already made it a few steps, but then the door closes loudly.

A voice shoots out from behind us. "Hey!"

I keep walking, but Trey turns to look.

"Hey," the voice repeats, with more urgency. The footsteps catch up with us. It's the man from before, with the stone-cold stare. He squints at me, deciding if he recognizes me as well. "Were you just inside there?" he demands.

"Um . . . where?" I ask, playing dumb.

He narrows his eyes at us. "Room 5403. It seems like you just came out of there."

My fingers sweat, still clinging to Trey's hand. All my cover stories evaporate from my head. "No," I say, my voice catching.

But Trey answers yes at the same time.

The officer searches my face with a hard glare. "Which is it?"

My mouth dries up, and Trey leans in toward the man, yanking me forward. "We were hunting dinosaurs," Trey says in a conspiratorial whisper.

I give the man an aren't-kids-the-darnedest shrug, and his suspicious expression falls away, his head dropping back in laughter. He smiles then, which completely transforms his face. "Dinosaurs, is that right?"

"Yeah," I say weakly. "We didn't find any down the whole hallway, though, did we?" I motion up and down the corridor, to drive home the point that we were *just* in the hallway, definitely not in her room.

"No dinosaurs," Trey says, with a somber headshake.

The man leans in toward him, cuffing his hand for a whisper. "I think there might be some in the Fun Factory," he says, winking at me.

"Nope," Trey answers staunchly. "We been there."

The man straightens up with a smile, looking back to his post. "You keep looking, my young man," he says. "You'll find them."

117

CHAPTER

eighteen

DAY 8

At Sea

The morning is already hot.

I'm running on the track, trying to quiet my mind, but my thoughts keep boomeranging back to the same question, looping like a soundtrack in my brain.

Ten thousand dollars. Ten thousand dollars. Ten thousand dollars.

Where would she get ten thousand dollars?

I want to talk to someone about it, but I can't even do that. *How do I know about the money? Oh, well, I snuck into her room and sort of opened the safe.* But still, I have to do something. Breathing hard, I enter the dark recess of the ship. The banging and clanging just adds to the chaos in my head. I exit the musty, dark ship into the sunlight again when an announcement comes over the speaker.

"Ladies and gentlemen, this is your captain speaking," comes the echoey, cheerful voice. Passengers pause whatever they are doing. People look up from books or stop swimming, staring at the speaker as if they might actually see the voice. I stop too, my breath ragged.

"We certainly appreciate your patience with our change in plans, and expect to return to Bermuda tomorrow."

This is followed by a general grumbling.

"*But* we will allow disembarking. And to show our appreciation, we are offering a free excursion for each family for up to a five-hundred-dollar value."

This news leads to a more appreciative murmur.

"Again, we certainly appreciate your patience, and hope to be sailing home very soon." A squeak of feedback punctuates the announcement. Then it's back to business as usual. Kids get back to their yelling and splashing. The steel drums start up some Rolling Stones song that my dad always sings in an embarrassing falsetto. I could just see Jade doing some kind of mock-funky dance to it. I touch her necklace, which I put on again today. I'm not sure why exactly, but I think I wanted to feel her with me.

I take a deep breath to dispel the sudden sadness falling over me and start running another lap. My toes burn with blisters.

Ten thousand dollars. Ten thousand dollars. Ten thousand dollars.

My feet pound a hollow sound onto the deck. Down below, I catch a glimpse of Joanie, reading a magazine with a piña colada, seemingly oblivious to the fact that her niece has vanished. An empty chair with a magazine holds Bob's place.

I head for the exit. I might as well go down there and find

out what Joanie knows. But as I reach the door, I nearly run into someone.

"Hello?" It's the inspector, the one who seemed to be in charge. "Isabel Mathers?" he asks me in that pseudo-English accent.

"Yes?" I answer.

"Inspector Curtis," he says with a wide, bright smile. His features seem rubbery, like they could change from angry to kind and back again in a second, which is probably a useful trait for a police officer. "We'd like to ask you some questions . . . about your friend."

"Jade?" I ask stupidly.

He nods, and my stomach churns with nerves. "Um, okay," I say.

"Great," he says, though I don't really feel like I had a choice. "Right this way, then." He motions for me to follow, and I do.

But I somehow feel like I'm walking to the gallows.

We wind our way down to a hidden labyrinth in the ship, a series of small rooms like the study rooms at my school library. I wonder if they took Bryce here too. The inspector opens the door to a hot lemon-yellow room. He motions for me to sit, then sits across from me. A fake LCD fish tank burbles on the wall, the same kind as in our stateroom, adding a certain absurdity to the proceedings.

"Just so you know," the inspector says, "you are not in any trouble here. We're doing a lot of interviews, and even more when we get back to Bermuda." He gives me a smile, but it drops when I don't return it. "We are just doing our best to find out what happened to your friend. Okay?"

"Okay," I say, not feeling any better about this. The back of my bra itches with dried sweat. I know I must smell disgusting.

"So . . . let's start with when you saw her last?" he asks, his pad open and pen at the ready.

"Tuesday night," I say, without having to think about it. "After the White Party, we went swimming."

"When was the exact time you saw her last?" he asks, writing.

My fingers start tapping out a rhythm. "Ten thirty, maybe? Ten forty-five?" Then my stomach lets out an embarrassing grumble. I didn't eat much before the run, and now I've missed lunch, so I am famished.

The inspector kindly ignores this, then consults his pad strewn with illegible scribbling. "Where was she going? Back to her room?"

I shake my head. "She got a message from Bryce to meet her. So, I assume she did. And . . . I never saw her again after that." The fish burble again, one staring right at me with its cartoony eyes. "I think he was the last one to see her alive. So . . ." I let the implication hang.

"Bryce says they were in his cabin . . . ," the inspector says, leaving an ellipsis for what they were doing. "And then she left. He didn't know where she went."

Ten thousand dollars. I found ten thousand dollars in her safe.

Inspector Curtis pushes his chair back from the table,

assuming a casual posture. "Is it possible she left the cruise after meeting with Bryce? Maybe . . . decided to go back into Bermuda for the night while you were still docked, for instance?" He searches me. "Did she mention this at all?"

My fingers tap again, and I pull my hand off the table to stop them. "No, she didn't tell me, but it's possible. I mean, she was kind of . . . adventurous."

The inspector briskly flips a sheet of his notebook. "Her aunt and uncle think she might have done so."

I think my mouth actually falls open. "That's not what they told me. They told me she was onboard. That she was sick with the flu. Quarantining, basically."

The inspector purses his lips. "Yes, they said they didn't want to worry you. But she had made insinuations to them that she was going to run away to Bermuda."

"Oh, okay," I answer, puzzled but on the other hand thrilled with this news. If she's in Bermuda, that means she's alive.

"Bryce had a different theory. He said she seemed quite depressed at times. He thinks it's possible that she jumped overboard," the inspector says with an off-putting smile. "What do you think?"

I think it would be very convenient for Bryce to give people that impression. "I don't think she was depressed."

Then he gives me an intense stare. The fish burble in the loud silence. Maybe he knows about the money.

"Where did you get your necklace?" he asks.

"My necklace?" My fingers automatically leap to touch it.

122

"Jade . . . loaned it to me." I stutter, though I don't know why it sounds like I'm lying when I'm not. "For the White Party."

Slowly, he nods. "Her aunt and uncle told me that it was missing. They thought it had been stolen."

I shake my head in embarrassment. "No, I swear," I say, again sounding like a liar. "She gave it to me. Loaned it to me, I mean."

Ten thousand dollars. She had ten thousand dollars.

His look is inscrutable. "People do that sometimes. Give away things that are special to them."

"Sure but . . ." I swallow. "It didn't seem like that. She said something kind of odd when she loaned me that necklace." I rub sweat from my forehead. "That I should keep it, if something should ever happen to her."

He stares ahead in concentration. The lines between his eyebrows indent into crevices. "And you took that to mean something . . . bad?"

Ten thousand dollars. She had ten thousand dollars.

I grip the edge of the table. "Did you talk to Diego yet? From the casino?"

The inspector eyes me. "You think he had something to do with it?"

My knee starts bouncing. "I saw him looking upset with her. He grabbed her arm. Maybe he has a history of violence." A school of silver fish pivots against the wall. "And I hate to say it but they seemed to be very . . ." I try to think of the least inflammatory description. "They seemed very close."

Inspector Curtis tilts his head. "I think in her mind, maybe, they were close." He scratches his knee below the Bermuda shorts. "In his mind, it was more of a schoolgirl crush thing."

I can't help but laugh at that one. "That's a lie. He seemed, like, creepy obsessed with her."

He shakes his head. "Diego says he didn't even see her that night," he says. His tone shuts me off. He didn't see her, end of story.

"But maybe he's lying," I say, drumming my knuckles on the table in frustration. I can't help but wonder why he wants to exonerate Diego so quickly. "I mean, did you see her Tik-Tok video?"

His blank stare tells me he did not.

"I'm not sure if it's Diego, but I think it could be. Or even Bryce maybe." I hand him the phone, and he watches it, just once. Then he looks up at me with a neutral expression. "What do you think?" I ask.

He raises his eyebrows. "I think she was on a cruise having fun with someone."

"Yeah, but . . . ," I insist, opening the video again. "Look at the time stamp." I point to it, and he humors me with a nod. "It was like three a.m. That could have been the last person to see her."

Ignoring me, the inspector keeps writing. Hunger gnaws at my stomach, and I try to ignore it. *Ten thousand dollars. Ten thousand—* "Did Diego say anything about money? Giving her money?" The words fly out before I can stop them.

"Money?" His head pops up from his pad. "Why do you ask that?"

"I don't . . . I just . . . wondered." I drop my eyes, knowing this sounds like a lie.

"Did she say something to you about money?" Inspector Curtis asks, leaning over the table now. "Was she going to use it in Bermuda?"

"No . . . I . . ." My fingers start tapping again. "I don't know." I want to tell him, but how can I? How exactly do I explain that I snuck into her room last night and went through her safe?

The inspector moves even closer to me. I can smell the starch of his uniform. "It feels like you're hiding something, Isabel. Is there something you would like to tell me?"

My mouth stays shut, the words fighting to get out.

"You won't be in trouble," he says, as if he means it. "We just want to get to the bottom of this. Find your friend. That's what you want too, right?"

I still don't speak.

"Isabel," Inspector Curtis says, more forcefully now. "If you know something, you have to tell me." His brown eyes bore into mine. "We're not playing games here. We need to—"

But before I can say a word, there's a loud scramble outside the door, and my father bursts into the room. Toni the cruise director follows on his heels, giving a shrug of apology to the inspector. My dad rushes to my side, putting a staunch arm around me. "She doesn't say one more word without a parent or her lawyer present. You got that?" He points a trembling finger at the inspector, his voice quaking with fury.

"Okay," Inspector Curtis says, backing off, putting up an

appeasing hand. "No need to get angry. I was just doing my job." He tries a collegial smile on him. "We are all on the same team, right? Trying to find out what happened to Jade."

My father's expression doesn't soften. "Come on, Izzy," he says, gently pulling my arm. "Let's go."

We march out then, and they don't try to follow us.

But I know the inspector won't leave it alone. He's not stupid. He knows I know something.

I'm not stupid either, though. I saw how quickly he let Diego off the hook. And I think he knows something too.

CHAPTER

nineteen

DAY 9

Return to Bermuda

As we walk down the hallway, my dad and I get a glimpse into another room. Jade's uncle sits in a chair with his head in his hands; another inspector appears to be grilling him.

Once we're out of earshot, my father turns to me. "You okay?"

"Yeah," I say. "Sort of."

He nods, and we walk the rest of the way to our room in silence, our flip-flops thunking down the hall. When we get to our room, it's empty.

"Trey's with the Guppies," he says, answering my unspoken question. "Mom's talking with Grayson."

I tilt my head. "Grayson?"

"Her partner from Rice and Rice." My dad glances down at his phone. "Then she's going to the consulate, I think. Anyway, they should be calling any minute."

The LCD porthole wave sways back and forth, and a striped yellow fish doing an about-face for the hundredth time. My dad flicks on the light, dispelling some of the gloom, and I crash onto the cot. The adrenaline holding me up during the interview has been completely spent.

With a sigh, my dad takes his keys, wallet, and phone out of his pockets and empties them onto the bed, sitting down heavily as well. "I'll just ask you this once," he says, "because I want you to know I believe you. And I trust you."

My brain flickers back to the biology test, shrinking at the memory. Maybe my dad shouldn't trust me so much.

"Do you know what happened to Jade?" he asks in a soft, measured voice. His eyes search me. I notice the slate-gray color, the exact shade of Trey's eyes.

"No," I answer. "I don't."

He pauses for just a second. "Okay," he says, and gives me a brisk nod. "Then we have nothing to worry about."

I nod back, but I'm not so sure about that.

He stands up and grabs my mom's flowery beach bag, which looks funny on him. "You hungry?" he asks. "I thought we could grab something from the Breakaway."

Since I could eat a horse right now, my answer is yes. So we head over to the poolside grill to grab some food. Sitting in the sun, I wolf down two hamburgers and every French fry on my plate. We sit then, digesting, while steel drums play "Little Drummer Boy" in the middle of April and my dad hums along. My mind keeps replaying the session with the inspector, analyzing things I should have or shouldn't have said. He didn't seem to take any of my insights seriously, but maybe that was just a front.

I think back to Bob in one of the rooms, his posture distressed.

Could she really be in Bermuda? Maybe I'm being paranoid, but every time I try to talk to her aunt and uncle, they seem to skitter away. I need to find out if that's what they really told the inspector, if they honestly believe she went to Bermuda. And even if they do, I gotta say, their niece went missing, and they've been romancing over candlelit dinners, sipping poolside drinks, catching the theater . . . In other words, they don't seem too broken up about it.

"I'm going to the computer room," I announce.

My dad stops humming and glances up. "You sure you're okay?" he asks.

"Yup," I say, grabbing my purse, antsy to start my own investigation.

He nods. "Okay," he says, looping the beach bag over his shoulder. "I'll see if your mom got anywhere with the consulate."

———

In the bustling computer room, I manage to find a seat without too much trouble.

My chair squeaks as random coughs and throat-clearing fill the room, along with whispering in the corner. Googling "Bob Gibson," a surprising number of hits pop up, so I add "New Jersey" to the search. I find a few tidbits, but nothing damning. He's smiling with his walrus mustache in one press release, having sold the most cars that month at Gerry's Volvo. He and Joanie smile in another picture in ill-fitting formal wear for a From Prison to Work benefit. Googling that organization brings up a low-rent website with their mission statement and some "success stories." I click on the photo album and scroll through some pictures, when Bob shows up again. He's leaning against jail bars, the outline of a prisoner shadowed behind him, captioned *Mr. Gibson shares a moment with a soon-to-be parolee.*

I sit back, studying the picture.

It's probably nothing. As Miranda would remind me, I might be reacting to my own prejudice toward prisoners. But something feels off about it. I keep digging, but nothing else emerges. The results for Joanie are patently boring. She appears to be an administrative assistant at a medical office. I get one hit from a "modern-day knitting circle," where she makes a scarf while gabbing it up with the ladies.

Yawn.

Checking my phone, I see about three minutes left in my allotted Wi-Fi time. So I open WhatsApp, and right away see a message from Luke.

I'm really sorry. But I just don't think we're right for each other. And just so you know, I'm dating Haley. I thought you should hear it from me first.

Right, I grumble to myself, after you let the entire school know on Instagram.

Anyway, I appreciate everything you did for me. I got an A on the test, so . . . that's a first. Haha. It helped out some of my friends too.

My breath stops. Some of his friends? The hamburgers churn in my stomach. He said he wouldn't show anyone. Jesus, now everyone will know. I'll get caught for sure.

I'm so stupid. So, so stupid.

See you around. I hope we can stay friends.

A mixture of outrage and fear pulses through me, and I

close the website. Not only does he show all his friends, but he has the audacity to end the message with the most generic of break-up lines possible. "I hope we can stay friends"? Yeah, that seems highly doubtful.

Standing up, I whip on my purse and stride out of the room. Miranda's right—he is an utter asshole. I can't wait to talk to Jade about it.

But then I remember, I can't talk to Jade.

———

I'm lying on a pool chair trying not to think about Luke.

It helped out some of my friends too.

I can't believe I was such an idiot.

"Marco!" someone yells.

"Polo!" others answer. A young girl twirls around with her eyes closed. With a sigh, I pick up *The Great Gatsby* and read a few paragraphs, but I can't concentrate on Nick and his First World problems. The tops of my feet sizzle, so I throw a towel on them and continue to ruminate.

"Marco!"

I consider going back to the computer room to let Luke know all the ways he can fuck himself. But then, I think, what's the use. "Polo!"

The image of Haley practically grinding on him dangles in my head, poking at something that's bothered me all along, even though I denied it. I've posted pictures of him, plenty of them—in his lacrosse gear, in his bow tie at the dance, semi-drunk at a party. But he has never once posted a picture of me. The truth was staring me in the face all along.

He never liked me all that much. "Marco!"

He was just using me. "Polo!"

I catch a whiff of my mom's freesia lotion as the girl twirls around again. "Hi," my mom says, sitting on the pool chair next to me. The wind blows the brim of her sun hat up.

"Hi," I answer. Everyone's going to find out about the test. Maybe I should just tell her now and get it over with.

"You want to talk about the meeting with the inspector?" she asks.

"Not right now," I say.

She nods, and takes her sun hat off, leaving her hair plastered to her forehead. "I have some not so terrific news."

I slap my book shut. More bad news, just great. "What?"

"We'll be in Bermuda tomorrow," she says. I raise my eyebrows, and she sighs. "They want to interview you . . . at the police station."

My heart twists. "I told them everything I know," I insist.

Except for one little thing.

She holds up a hand. "I know, I know. And I tried my best to get us out of it. But the laws are different here. And they have a low threshold for arrest if we don't comply."

"Arrest?" I feel myself starting to hyperventilate.

She puts her hand on my arm. "I shouldn't have put it quite like that. No one's arresting you. And we'll be there with you, plus one of the partners over Skype. So . . . you don't have to worry about anything."

Right, I think. Except getting dumped by Luke, being expelled for cheating, and finding my missing friend. "Marco!"

"Polo!" Nothing at all to worry about.

CHAPTER

twenty

We have a solemn meal at the ship's fifties-themed dinner, which features pink neon, an old Wurlitzer jukebox, and pictures of sock hops, Elvis Presley, and Doris Day on the walls. After eating my Rocket burger (which tasted exactly like the Breakaway Café burgers), I am mercifully excused.

"Oh," my mom says as I stand up from the stiff red booth. "We're in Bermuda now. So you should have cell signal if you want to use it. From the international plan. There's one silver lining, right?"

"Sure," I say. I know she's just trying to make me feel better about tomorrow's interrogation. I walk out, passing a waitress carrying a tray of melting sundaes in those fancy metal dishes.

When I get to the room, a towel molded into a swan sits on the bed with its neck askew. I sit down on the squeaky cot, utterly exhausted. My muscles feel like they won't even hold me up, like I'm a puppet about to collapse. When I lie down, though, I don't feel sleepy, just nervous.

Tomorrow morning. I'm going to have to tell them about the money.

There's no way around it.

Anxiety roiling in me, I sit back up. I rip open a chocolate mint from one of the pillows, toss it into my mouth, and turn on the television to take my mind off things. But I can find only three channels with poor reception, one of which is a boring soccer game where no one scores. Three other channels essentially run ads about the ship and the excursions, complete with multicultural families smiling and swimming around (with no sign of sullen teenagers or tantruming toddlers). Then I remember what my mom said about the cell signal. So I turn off the TV and turn on my cell data *finally*, ready to TikTok to my heart's content. And maybe I can text Miranda and see if Luke's done anything douchey lately. Or I can just go ahead and text Luke myself to tell him what an asshole he is.

But a text message pops on the screen before I can check social media.

I don't recognize the number at first, but then I realize it's a text from her New Jersey area code. My breathing stops.

I'm really sorry. I just couldn't take it anymore. Tell my aunt and uncle that I love them. See you on the other side. . . .

Love, Jade

CHAPTER

twenty-one

I don't sleep.

It's 3:45 a.m. Less than three hours before I'm seeing the inspector, but my brain is on fire. Could it be?

No, it couldn't be.

It's impossible. It can't be her.

I check out the time stamp—the night she went missing. I just never got it because my stupid cell data has been off. So, it could have been a suicide note that she sent that night. But would she really *text* a suicide note?

The thing is, I could actually see her texting a suicide note.

The ocean sways beneath me. The sensation should be soothing, lulling, but feels unsteady and destabilizing instead, as if the ocean wants to pitch me out of my bed. The dips and rises match the churning in my brain. I hold on tight to the cold metal rails on the cot.

Is it possible?

Maybe Bryce was right—that she was depressed, and she just didn't show it around me. Sure, she was sad about the situation with her mom. She couldn't stand Bob and Joanie. But she wasn't, like, kill-yourself depressed.

Then again, if she was high on ketamine, maybe her inhibitions were gone. Or maybe she was hallucinating something, or on a really bad trip. But then how would she write such a coherent note?

And she wouldn't even say that anyway. That's the biggest thing against this being her. She would never say *tell my aunt and uncle that I love them.* Maybe her mom, but not her aunt and uncle. Never.

It can't be her. It's just too convenient, too easy. Anyone could have her phone. Anyone could have sent that. No need to copy her handwriting or sneak a note into her room. Poof, just send a text. And they would think I would get it right away, and the case would be solved.

The boat lifts and drops. I imagine us cresting on a huge wave, the size of a building. My family sleeps peacefully, Trey sucking his thumb in his bed, my dad snoring and my mom as silent as a stone. I want to flip on the lights and scream, *Wake up! Help me. Tell me what to do.* But I can't. I can't tell them. Because they'll just believe the text message right away. They won't second-guess it for a minute. Just like the inspector won't.

And maybe I wouldn't have, had I gotten it right away.

But I didn't.

And in the meantime, I've found ten thousand reasons why she didn't kill herself.

CHAPTER

twenty-two

DAY 10

Bermuda

I must have fallen asleep at some point, because the blare of my father's alarm wakes me up at five freaking o'clock. The room swells with tension, while my mom puts on her most professional outfit and I do the same. As Trey sleeps and my dad watches with worry, a gray, sick feeling overcomes me.

See you on the other side.

No, no. It's impossible.

A bright knock blasts through the room. "Hello, Captain here," he calls out.

With a sigh, my mom opens the door, where he stands tall and upright.

"Are you ready?" he asks with his ever-present smile, as if we're going to Disney World and not an interrogation. We grunt our assent, and he leads us down the gangplank and over to the station, keeping up an annoyingly peppy banter the whole way. Though he probably wakes up by four a.m., so this is like noon to him.

"Gonna be a hot one today," he says, bounding ahead in that confident way of his. "I suppose, it's always hot this time of year."

"Mmph," my mom says, sounding the way I feel.

"You'll see some amazing architecture, too," he adds, which he pronounces *a-my-zing.*

His shoes crunch on the pavement as we cross the street. The heat assaults me, sweat already forming under my lacy shirt. "You can't miss St. Peter's Church while you're here."

It takes everything not to yell at him. *Do you understand this isn't the Hop-On, Hop-Off city excursion? My friend is missing, and I don't know what happened to her. I'm meeting with the police. We are not visiting freaking St. Peter's Church.* "Okay," he says, finally depositing us in the police station where Inspector Curtis waits. "Have a nice—" He looks momentarily flummoxed and just gives us an awkward wave goodbye. Oh yes, I'm sure we'll have a grand old time.

———

We are seated in the pink (like everything else in Bermuda) interview room at a scuffed table, my mom and me on one side and the inspector across from us. The chairs are wooden too, and hard. I hate these kinds of chairs. My bony butt gets sore after ten minutes. We prop up a tablet to Skype with Grayson, our lawyer and my mom's partner. We are connecting to him when I notice it.

Right there on the desk. A manila envelope.

My mouth goes dry.

The money, with my fingerprints all over it. I don't have to tell him. He knows already.

"You okay?" the inspector asks me, while my mom watches me with concern.

I nod too forcefully, making me look anything but okay. "Could I have some water?" I ask, my voice squeaking.

"She needs water," my mom butts in, as if I need a translator.

"Yes, of course," the inspector says, motioning to one of his men by the door, who runs to get it. "I see you are not wearing Jade's necklace today."

"No," I say. The air-conditioning chills me, my arms pebbling with goose bumps.

He smiles, and I'm not sure if this means something or not. Inspector Curtis taps his pen on his paper, the sound continuous and unnerving. Tap, tap, tap, tap, tap . . .

See you on the other side.

I blink hard, to make the thought go away. I try not to look at the manila envelope. Is it the money? Maybe it's something else that doesn't have to do with the case at all.

"Thank you," he says, "so much for coming. As you know, I'm still trying to find out what happened to your friend. And I'm hoping you can provide some explanations."

"Of what exactly?" Grayson asks, through the tablet, appearing strangely like a disembodied head.

"We'll get to that," the inspector says.

"What about the Bermuda theory?" I ask, my tongue sticking to the roof of my mouth. "You thought she might be here."

He shakes his head with an air of finality. "We have looked everywhere. Unless she is *extremely* good at hiding, she is not in Bermuda."

A swift sadness swells in me, though I hadn't even realized I was clinging to this hope.

I'm sorry. I just couldn't take it anymore.

Maybe I should just show him. But there's no way she killed herself. It's impossible.

"What about her aunt and uncle? They might be lying," I say, licking my dry lips. "They've been avoiding me. And her uncle seems to have some strange connections that I—"

"Her aunt and uncle are not suspects," the inspector says. "They were dancing in the YOLO Club all night."

I visualize the club. Lots of glossy dark furniture, mirrors, women in low-cut leopard-skin tops. I can't picture knitting Joanie in the YOLO Club all night.

The guard comes back with a can of ginger ale, which I can't stand. But I can't exactly put in a special order. I open it and take a drink, the lukewarm ale fizzing unpleasantly in my mouth. But at least my tongue can move.

"Bryce and Diego," the inspector says, as if reading my mind. "Alibis for both," he says. "Diego was working the casino all night. This has been verified by . . ." He consults his notes. "A bouncer who works there. Sergei."

Right, I think. And no way he would be covering for his friend.

"And Bryce's friend"—he again turns to his notes, the papers flipping—"Caleb," he says, "can vouch that they spent hours playing video games in the Hang Out."

"He never said anything to me about that," I say. I can't believe Caleb would lie like that. But then again, he would do anything for his hero. I shift in the chair, my left leg going numb.

"So what do you think happened?" my mom asks the inspector.

He pauses, a smile sliding onto his face. "Actually, I was hoping Isabel could tell me that."

The ginger ale can feels sweaty in my hand. "I don't know." I sneak a look at the envelope. Does he think I had something to do with it? *See you on the other side.* Maybe I should show him. But then he'd stop looking for the truth. I mean, honestly, he's already stopped. He's taking these lame-ass alibis without challenging them in the least. Maybe he was given orders to wrap things up. Or maybe . . . he doesn't want the truth coming out.

"Isabel?" Inspector Curtis asks again, an edge to his voice.

"My client already stated that she doesn't know," Grayson says.

"Do you know what Jade was wearing the night she went missing?" the inspector asks, again trying to disarm me with a non sequitur.

"Um, a dress with blousy sleeves. White, obviously." I think back. Blond, impossibly shiny hair. Blue eyes that looked like they had storm clouds in them sometimes. A smile that was happy and sad.

See you on the other side.

He gives a sober nod, then carefully puts on blue gloves,

stretching each one with the squeak of a rubber balloon. He opens the manila envelope and pours the contents onto the table.

"Do you recognize this, Isabel?" he asks.

My mom gasps, but it takes me a second to register what I'm seeing. In a clear bag, the muddy sleeve of her white dress, torn and stained with blood. Her thin white belt, the pearls cracked and scratched.

And the diamond necklace.

A flush spreads over me in an instant, head to toe. I can't catch my breath.

"Izzy?" my mom asks. Her voice comes out funny.

"What's happening?" Grayson asks.

What's happening? What's happening? What's happening?

The words keep echoing and I stand up. I'm losing my mind. I have to get out of here now. I can't stay in here for another second. I take a step, but the floor turns to jelly.

And I collapse.

CHAPTER

twenty-three

The ceiling is pink too, which I only know because I'm lying on the floor, staring up at it.

A sea of faces hover over me, including my mom's. I start to sit up, feeling nauseous.

"Take your time," my mom says, holding my hand. I touch the back of my sore head, finding a tender goose egg. I moan without meaning to, and someone hands me a glass of water.

"I'm telling you right now," my mom says to the room, in her angry-mom voice, "if she has a concussion, you'd better believe we're going to—"

"Mom," I say, through dry lips. "It's okay." My voice sounds off. Everything seems wavy and hazy but normal at the same time. My mom helps me back to my chair, and I sit back down with rubbery legs. Once seated, my head starts pounding. I clutch my hair, seeing the envelope with her muddy items again.

Then, like an idiot, I start crying. Tears crawl into my eyes, and my nose starts running. The clothes snuff out the little part of me that couldn't believe she could really be dead.

I'm sorry. I just couldn't take it anymore.

"I think we need a break here," Grayson says, the talking head forgotten on the table.

"Yes," my mom says. "We need to get back on the ship and get my daughter some medical attention."

The inspector appears regretful. "I didn't mean to cause any harm. You understand that I had to see Isabel's reaction to—"

"Wait," I say, then I pause.

Everyone looks at me. Their faces freeze in time, staring, waiting for me to say more.

The silence solidifies.

"I have to show you something," I say, and pull out my phone.

My mom furrows her eyebrows, and Grayson pipes up. "Perhaps I should have a discussion with my client here."

But it's too late. The message looms on my screen, and I get the weird feeling that it's alive somehow, and I've been trapping it in my phone. The inspector reads it, not breathing.

"What's going on?" Grayson asks, sounding aggravated. I point the screen toward the tablet and watch him take it in. "Oh," he says, all the aggravation gone.

"It was sent two days ago," the inspector says with a hint of reproof.

"Yes," I admit. "But I didn't get it until yesterday, I swear. My cell service was off." I throw my mom an accusatory look, but she just nods.

The inspector starts tapping his pen again, the sound driving into my head, then he exhales, a sympathetic look on his face. "Okay, Isabel. I can understand why you were reluctant to tell me. You didn't want to believe it was real."

"That's the thing." I bite my lip, knowing this won't go over well. "I'm still not sure that it even is."

The statement is followed by an embarrassed, piteous silence.

"She wouldn't say that," I insist, my voice rising in desperation. " 'Tell my aunt and uncle that I love them'?" My temples throb, and I rub them. "She wouldn't say that."

"It was sent from her phone," the inspector says. He is trying to sound understanding, but there's a note of impatience.

"But someone could have her phone," I answer.

"I'm sorry, Isabel," Inspector Curtis says, his arms crossed now, apparently having made his decision. Suicide. End of investigation, onto the next case.

"This is why I didn't want to show you," I murmur.

He sighs. "Isabel, I understand you don't want to believe this. And it's hard to make sense of it. But unfortunately, she would not be the first to commit suicide this way. It can be . . ." he pauses. "Impulsive. Right? You don't plan it, but you're very upset about something and then . . ."

"You jump," I say. *See you on the other side.*

His expression takes on a mournful cast. "Yes."

My mom pats my shoulder, tears in her eyes. "I'm sorry, Isabel."

I don't say anything, because I don't want to start crying again, and my head is killing me. But then I consider the note again. Really, the message is so generic, anyone could have come up with it. Except for the part about Bob and Joanie, which she wouldn't even say.

"What about the safe?" I ask.

The inspector blinks, his body becoming too still. "The safe?"

"Yes. Did . . . did you find anything in there?" My voice trembles. "I'm pretty sure she had money in there. Did someone take it?"

His features harden. "No. The safe was empty," he says, each word steely, leaving no room for doubt. "I had the officers run through the whole room with a fine-tooth comb. Including the safe. They said there was nothing there. And I believe them."

"Okay," I say. The officers might have taken the money, or Inspector Curtis did. But there's no way I can bring it up without revealing I snooped in there.

After an awkward pause, my mom says, patting my arm, "I'm sure Izzy is just trying to be thorough."

"Yes," Grayson says. "I don't think we need to—" But then the screen goes black. We stare at it a moment, as if Grayson might pop back on there again. But he doesn't.

"The battery probably died," Inspector Curtis says, not seeming too bothered.

My mom takes in a breath. "Well, I think we're just about done here anyway so . . ."

"Yes," the inspector says, a sympathetic smile returning. A smile I don't trust.

"Listen," he says, handing me his business card. "If you

146

need anything, call me. Even if you're just upset and want to talk. Okay?"

Out of politeness, I nod. But I plan to toss that thing as soon as I get to the room.

He claps his hands together then, with an air of relief. "Let's call the captain, shall we?"

CHAPTER

twenty-four

A banging noise wakes me up, and I open my eyes in the dark room. The goose egg from my fainting spell at the police station aches. Slowly, I sit up, my mouth pasty. I check my cell phone, which says one p.m. Apparently I have accidentally taken a three-hour nap. I also see the What App message that woke me up, from Miranda.

Hey girl (womyn),

What's up? Hope you're having a blast in the sun. You're probably a tan goddess right now. I'm pale as ever but I wanted to tell you . . . I MET SOMEONE! At Barnes and Noble. Her name is Rosie (she/her) and she's supercute and smart and funny. Pink hair, the cutest nose ring. We talked a little and exchanged numbers, and then she texted me first!

Oh, and one more thing.

There's a rumor going around about you and Luke. I know it's a total lie, and you would never do something like that. But I wanted to let you know anyway in case you hear about it. People are saying that you guys cheated on the biology test and—

I close the message.

If she knows, everyone knows. The school has a zero-tolerance cheating policy, which means I'll be expelled. So then I can be a loser at another school, without even my best friend there.

Standing up, I flip on the light, which stings my eyes. I squint and see a note from my parents on *Crown Jewel* paper.

Thought you could use some rest. Let us know when you wake up.

I put the note back, sitting back on the cot.

I heard a rumor. I heard a rumor.

I flip off the light and lie back down. I don't want to be awake right now. But seconds later, a cruise chat ping goes off, startling me. "Can't these people just let me sleep?" I moan. Glancing at the chat, I think for a second that it'll be Jade, then remember, with a pit in my stomach. It can't be Jade.

It's Bryce. *The inspector told me about what they found.*

Sorry, I message back.

Meet?

I pause. No, I really don't want to meet up with him right now. But I suppose he deserves some explanation.

Where? I ask.

At the pool.

Be there in 10.

———

Looking around, I see Bryce in the hot tub. He catches my eye and gives a half wave, and I wave back. My head throbs, and I don't think a big session in the hot tub will help, but I don't really have a choice.

As I climb into the hot tub, a film of sunscreen coats the water, and bubbles creep around my legs. A middle-school-aged boy in a white sun shirt keeps splashing his friend while his mom reads a magazine, ignoring him. Bryce nods a hello, leaning back with his chest out of the water, and aviators on. I've already caught a bunch of girls (and women) gawking at him. To his credit, he doesn't seem to notice.

"Where's Caleb?" I ask. I'm surprised he let Bryce out of his sight.

"I don't know. Doing some Hang Out thing."

"Oh," I say.

"Everyone knows about it, you know," Bryce says. "It's all over the ship, that her stuff was found, that she jumped."

I don't say anything.

"When were you planning on telling us?" he asks, muted anger in the words. "That she texted you."

"I told the inspector," I say, "I didn't get the text until yesterday morning. My stupid mom won't let me keep my cell service on." Tears spring to my eyes, and I turn away, embarrassed.

We sit in silence for a bit, until the kid starts splashing again, and I move away from him.

"Anyway, I'm not sure I even believe it."

Bryce shoots me a look, hard to decipher under his sunglasses. "Why not?"

I pause. If he's involved, maybe I shouldn't tell him my suspicion. But I decide to take a chance. "It seems weird, doesn't it? To text instead of write a note?"

He shrugs at this. "Maybe."

"And she said something weird. That I should tell her aunt and uncle she loves them. You think she'd even say that?"

He looks at me again. A warped version of myself is reflected in the mirror of his sunglasses. "Can I see it?" he asks.

I grab my phone from the ledge, where I stashed it away from the water, and pull up the message. I hand it to him, careful to shield it from the splashing kid.

"It's her number," he comments.

"Yeah, obviously," I say. "But anyone could have her phone."

He purses his lips. "That's the only text?"

I nod, and he hands me back the phone. The kid in the white shirt pushes a button, ramping up the bubbles. The high-pitched whine of the motor makes it hard to hear. "Do you really think she was that depressed?" I ask. I have to practically yell to be heard. "Do you think she would do that?"

Bryce takes off his sunglasses for a second, revealing his eyes, rimmed with red. From crying? "People don't always advertise that they're gonna kill themselves. They just do it. And she gave you her necklace, right? They say they do that . . ." His voice fades off. He puts his sunglasses back on.

I swallow back tears and sit up in the tub, my skin stinging with the heat.

Then the middle-schooler goes for one more mountainous splash, hitting everyone in the tub.

"Kid," Bryce snarls at him, grabbing his wrist. "Stop. With. The. Splashing."

The boy turns as white as his shirt. "Sorry," he murmurs, tears filling his eyes. Magazine Mom finally notices him. She gives Bryce a dirty look, which he ignores, though he has let the kid's wrist go.

"Come on, Tyler," she says, and gathers him out of the hot tub.

Bryce leans back again, folding his arms as if nothing happened. As if he didn't just lose his temper, snapping in an instant.

Like maybe he did with Jade.

My head throbbing and dizzy, I climb out of the hot tub. I can't stand being in there with him, not knowing. Suicide is an easy answer, and everyone wants the case to go away. But she's not a case. She was my friend.

My phone dings with a cruise text.

Where are you honey? Is everything okay? We've been worried about you.

I'm fine, I answer. *Be back in room soon.*

But I have something to do first.

———

I walk down the hall of Deck Four, wet and chilled from the air-conditioning, my head hurting. Still, I plow ahead. I need to look in her room. Maybe I can find that journal to give me some answers. But that means two things: (1) sweet-talking the guard to get in, and (2) praying that Bob and Joanie didn't already take it.

But when I get to her door, not only is there no guard, there's not even a chair. So that takes care of problem number one.

Then I pull the *J* key from my other bag and realize I have a new problem. The lock has probably been changed. With a deep breath of anticipation, I put the key in, and the green light comes on.

Yes. Thank God.

In a way, I'm shocked that they haven't changed it by now. But then again, they don't seem too concerned with the "crime scene" anymore.

Doing a quick survey of the room, I see most of the stuff has been searched already. A fine gray fingerprinting dust covers various spots in the room, a few books, the edge of her desk, a pair of flip-flops. The sampling seems haphazard, but perhaps there's a logic I can't decipher. In such a small room, every area would be a high traffic area for thousands of different passengers, not to mention staff. They'd be lucky to get one significant fingerprint. A *Crown Jewel* towel lies neatly folded on the floor by the closet. Since Jade kept her room even messier than mine, I doubt that was her doing.

Checking under the bed, I find her shoes and luggage. I drag her suitcase out, a stained, beat-up pink bag that would be easy to pick out in baggage claim. Smoothing my fingers over the inside, I find it completely empty except for a Chapstick stuck in a corner. I shove the bag back under the bed, moving on to the shoes. I stuff my hand into her ratty Chuck Taylors and newish black heels. Nothing. Rifling through the drawers reveals a plethora of bikinis, some sweet Victoria's Secret bras, and a mess of tank tops, shorts, and summery pj's.

In the bathroom, there's metallic dust over a handprint on the curtain, and on the white sink as well. The garbage bin has been emptied, the contents likely examined at the start of the investigation. Just for kicks, I open up the Tylenol bottle to find—surprise, surprise—Tylenol.

Stepping back into the room, I do one last visual sweep of the room. No journal. It might still be in her book bag, but I don't see that anywhere. I try to think where I might hide a journal . . . Maybe a high shelf or under the bed. I sweep the shelf and look under the bed again, to no avail. I open the deep drawer of her nightstand once more, just in case I missed anything. The wood squeaks as I open it, the contents sliding around. A bible (doubtfully hers), three eye-liners of various shades of black, a makeup brush with the hairs splayed out, a shimmery rose lip gloss and a cherry-red lipstick. So, nothing of note.

I'm shutting the drawer when something else catches my eye.

I wasn't even going to bother with it, because it's hardly worth noticing—the ubiquitous and lowly package of sanitary pads. No fingerprint dust on this one.

Where would I hide something, if I wanted no one to look there, especially men?

I stuff my hand into the large package, and my fingers feel a boxy book. With a smile, I pull it out, the paisley journal. I tuck the journal under my arm and start to shut the drawer when I notice something about one of the pads, puffy with bright purple plastic wrapping.

But the shape seems off, bulging on one side. So I open the pad, the wrapper crinkling. And nestled inside sits the baggie with the ketamine pills.

And then I notice something else.

There are three ketamine pills, not four.

CHAPTER

twenty-five

Fortunately, no one's in our room yet. Lying on the cot, a spring digs into my elbow as I open the journal. Thanks to the Motrin in my mom's dopp kit, my headache has dulled to a soft hum. The Motrin calls to mind the other pills, the ketamine. Three instead of four, which means that Bryce is probably right—she was high that night. I flip through the first few pages.

She doesn't write a whole lot, mostly doodles.

I think of my own journal, with pages of tortured exposition on whether Luke does or doesn't like me, and random thoughts, little poems. Then more recently, frantic scribbling weighing the pros and cons of cheating on the test. Of course, the pros were a mirage, something I should have known all along.

But Jade doesn't fill her pages up with questions. She has a blunter style. Like Hemingway, but less misogynistic.

This cruise sucks.

That's the first page, with a drawing of a huge ship and smoke billowing out the top, in which she's inserted the words *I am stupid*, as if it's a conversation bubble.

The next page:

Met cute boy, Bryce. Think he's into me. Also, Izzy is cool.

Cruise might not blow as much as I thought it would.

I can't help but smile at my brief description, which may be the only time anyone has referred to me as cool. This one has a random smiley doodle. Next page.

Made out with Bryce. Extremely hot. He talked about sex . . . but I'm not sure.

Reading the journal, I almost feel like she's here again. Like I could just cruise chat her about something she said. I flip to the next page with a sigh.

This page has an unmistakable caricature of Bob with his tell-tale mustache and Joanie looking both sour and worried, her expression caught perfectly. Underneath she has written:

I FUCKING HATE BOB AND JOANIE!!!!!

Checking their picture, I notice another thing—their eyes crossed out with *X*s.

The door clicks open then, and I jump up, twinging my elbow. I shove the journal under my pillow.

"Hi, hon," my mom says, in her singsong mom voice. "I'm sorry I've been out. I had to check in with the embassy again." She tosses her flowery beach bag onto the bed, a blue canister of sunscreen spilling out. "What are you up to?"

"Nothing," I say, trying to look innocent. "Just hanging. Taking a nap."

"With all the lights on?" Her eyes crinkle in suspicion. "Didn't you just take a nap a couple hours ago?"

"Yeah, well," I say. "I wanted another one."

She backs off immediately, looking chastened. "I know.

156

You've been through a lot. And you were up early." She sits on her bed, leaning toward me. "How are you feeling? How's your head?"

I shrug. "Okay, I guess."

"We have disco night for dinner," she says, reaching over and chucking my shoulder. "Sound good?"

"Disco?" I ask. "That was, like, a hundred years ago."

"Wait till I tell your dad that one," she says, chortling. She stands up then, heading to the mirror and frowning. "You don't have to dress up. We don't even have to go. I just want us to eat as a family."

Translation: *I want to keep my eye on you.*

The door whirs again, and Trey bursts through, followed by my exhausted-looking dad.

"ZiZi," Trey bellows joyously and barrels right into me.

"Hey," my mom scolds. "Your sister has a headache. Don't hurt her."

"Sorry," he says, his expression genuinely apologetic. Then he climbs on top of me like a puppy. Toddlers do not understand personal space. "Hide seek?" he asks. "Find dinosaurs?"

My mom looks at us in the mirror, running fingers through her tangled hair. "What do you mean, find dinosaurs?"

"Yeah," he squeals, "in the room!"

"What room?" she asks.

"It's a game we were playing," I mutter. "Maybe later, Trey."

"Stop bothering your sister," my dad chides, taking his Princeton baseball cap off. He turns to me, his salt-and-pepper

157

hair stuck to his head. "You gonna get showered for dinner? I can go when you're done."

"Sure," I say. The journal under my pillow calls to me. I feel an almost magnetic pull to start reading again. Turning away from my parents, I grab my backpack and put it on my bed.

"So . . . ," my mom mumbles. "What's Trey gonna wear?"

She rifles through his drawer, and I take the opportunity to stuff the journal into my backpack. Acting nonchalant, I carry the bag with me to the bathroom and shut the door. I turn on the shower and sit back on the toilet seat, grabbing the journal as the faucet roars.

They don't give a shit about me. All they care about is Gram's money. And they're not even using it on me!!

I know why we're even on this dumb cruise in the first place. Uncle Bob has a little secret. And I'm gonna tell Gram.

I turn the next page as softly as I can. Steam fills the room. *Little secret . . .* What little secret? But the next page carries no mention of Bob and Joanie.

Diego's cute, in a bad-boy kind of way. Kinda old, though. We'll see. . . .

The edge of the page wrinkles in the steam. On one side, she's drawn a little rough sketch of Diego, getting his prominent eyebrows just right, and on the other side, she's drawn Bryce, with watchful eyes, his floppy hair falling into them.

Diego keeps talking to me. Bryce saw and got pissed. Got right in my face and yelled at me, asked if we were serious or not. I acted all fuck you, but when he walked away I was shaking. He gave me that mean look. How boyfriend #5 looked right before he punched Mom in the face.

158

An angry knocking blasts through the door, and I nearly drop the journal.

"Are you almost done in there?" my mom asks, sounding annoyed.

"Yup!" I yell, and shove the journal back in my bag.

Climbing into the burning hot shower, I think back to the words about Bryce and Diego. And the picture of her aunt and uncle looming on the page, both bumbling and menacing.

With Xs through their eyes.

CHAPTER

twenty-six

Disco night means platform shoes, garish glittery outfits, and animal prints everywhere. Each table has a little disco ball, which Trey has already somehow dismantled, while the Bee Gees play on a loop over the speakers. My parents act like this is a normal dinner, like every other night. No one talks about the interrogation this morning. No one talks about the text. Or Jade. And I just want to get back to the room to read the journal. When cheesecake comes around, I figure I've put in enough family time and get ready to leave. But the captain swings by.

"Hello. How are we all tonight?" He glances around the room, looking dapper in his uniform. "This is something, huh?" he says, though I'm sure he's done a hundred of these dinners already.

"Oh yes," my father says. "Very festive."

"How was your day in Bermuda?" he asks, a spark in his voice as if he just remembered. "Did you get to see the church?"

"Um, no," my mom says with a tight smile.

I just stare at him. I mean, how clueless is this guy?

"Oh right," he says, his expression sheepish. Then he leans down with his hands on his knees, table level. "I was wondering if you wanted a tour of the captain's quarters one of these nights?"

My dad wipes his chin with a napkin. "Sure, sure," he says. "That would be terrific."

"Wonderful," he says in his hearty voice. He claps my father on the back so hard he could spit out his food. The captain ruffles Trey's hair. "I bet this little guy would love it."

Coming off a grape lollipop high, Trey barely deigns to look at him. Clearly, this charm offensive is an attempt to make up for everything, especially since my mom's a lawyer. As if a little tour of his stupid office would mean anything.

"I need some air," I say, standing up.

My mom stands too. "I'll come," she says.

"No," I snap, then take a deep breath, calming my voice. "I'm fine. You can . . . stay here . . . Really, I'm fine."

I stride along the deck—where couples embrace against the railing and people stargaze with binoculars—and hurry back to the room, when I see Bob and Joanie standing in front of their room, about to go in. We all stop, frozen. I have a disturbing flash image of them with Xs through their eyes. "Hi," I say. "Can we talk for a second? About Jade? I just wanted to—"

"No," Joanie says. Rosy spots appear on her checks. "We already told the inspector everything. Now just leave us in peace." She opens the door, and I don't know how or why, but I move in front of them, blocking their entrance.

Joanie looks at me, her eyes flaring with outrage and

shock, while Bob crosses his arms over his belly, staring at the floor.

"Do you think she really killed herself?" I ask, which comes out as a demand more than a question.

Joanie's expression softens. "Well . . . ," she says.

"She blamed herself," Bob says in a low, gravelly voice. "For her mom being in jail."

"Because her mom got high with Jade's money," I say, remembering this.

"Not just that," he says, shaking his head. "Jade's the one who called nine-one-one when her mom wouldn't wake up. Which of course was the right thing to do. But then social services got involved and . . ."

He doesn't have to finish the sentence. I think back to that night in the pool under the stars. *What's the worst thing you've ever done?* Maybe she had wanted to unburden herself. But I wasn't a true friend at all. I lied straight to her face.

"One more thing," I say before moving out of their way. I think of her words in the journal. *I know his little secret.* "Did you know she had ten thousand dollars in her safe?"

Neither answers for a second.

"Ten thousand dollars?" Bob winds his mustache around his finger, coiling it tight. "We don't know anything about ten thousand dollars."

"No, we sure don't," Joanie says, her voice hard as metal again. She folds her arms over her wide chest. "Now, I think it's time for you to leave."

———

I fully expect everyone to be there when I get to the room, but my mom messages me that she's talking to the lawyer again, and Trey and Dad are at the arcade.

Thanking God for small miracles, I dig out the journal.

I open it to yet another shocking entry.

Diego gave me a DIAMOND necklace. Had to be superexpensive. Way more than he makes. So he's got some side deal going on.???

So Diego gave her the necklace? How on earth could he afford that? I hear thumping down the hall and slap the journal shut, my heart galloping. But then the footsteps keep going, along with the squeaking of a cleaner's cart. Taking a breath, I open the journal again.

I like Diego, kind of. He's obviously into me. I put the necklace in the safe so my aunt and uncle can't get to it.

I put my finger on that sentence, remembering an earlier page, when she said her uncle was wasting all her money. She was actually afraid they would steal from her.

Bryce would kill me if he knew it was from Diego. He asked me for the tenth time if I really even liked him. Because "it seems like all you care about is Diego." No idea where he's getting that from.

"Because he's an insecure asshole," I mutter.

He said if I don't want him, he'll find someone else. Ha. Good luck with that. Most of the other girls are younger than him, and for whatever reason he hates Izzy. So, yeah, good luck.

I stop reading. Bryce hates me? Really? My cheeks feel hot. I guess this is why you don't read other people's journals. You might not like what you find. I must not have been paying attention, because suddenly I hear the key in the slot and shove the journal under my bed again.

The door opens, and my mom swoops in.

I arrange my face in a smile. "Where's Dad and Trey?" I ask.

"One more game of Whac-a-Mole." She plucks off her heels. "I think your dad is secretly playing Pac-Man, to be honest," she says with a chuckle.

I fake a chuckle back.

Then my mom sits directly across from me on her bed. "How are you doing?" she asks. Not, like, in a casual way. In an earnest way, the way the social worker at school would ask.

"Okay," I say.

She waits for more, then ventures in again. "I know you've been through a lot lately, hon. And I just want you to know, we're here for you. We're always here for you."

"Yeah," I say lightly.

She takes a deep breath. "You'd tell us, right?" she asks, a tremor in her voice. "If you were very unhappy." She slips off the bed so she's at my level, clinging to my hand. "You can tell us. Anything. Okay?"

The words get stuck in my mouth. I *could* tell her. I could tell her about Luke, the cheating, the ketamine. Even the journal. I look up at her worried, expectant eyes and squeeze her hand back.

"Yes," I say with a swallow. "I would tell you."

CHAPTER

twenty-seven

DAY 11

Depart Bermuda, Returning to New York City, At Sea

I dream there's a rattlesnake under my pillow and wake up gasping.

Then I feel the vibration of my alarm, which I set for five a.m. It's really freaking early, but I wanted to get some reading in before the family woke up. Not wasting any time, I pull out the journal again. I stifle a yawn and turn the page to a doodle of ocean waves.

Bryce was seasick tonight so he didn't want to hang. Which was fine by me by the way. The other night we were fooling around, but he was going too far and I pushed him away and said didn't want to and he got kind of moody and said, "I bet you're fucking Diego, though." I told him to fuck off and got up to leave but he grabbed my hand and said, "I'm sorry," like a hundred times. He was crying, so I think he meant it. So I forgave him. For now anyway.

I shake my head with fury. That guy reads like Abusive Red Flags 101. I probably should tell her. . . .

But I bite my lip. Of course I can't tell her.

Maybe I'll have sex with him. But I don't know. I want my first time to be with someone really special. Bryce is hot. But special? Not sure about that.

I reread the page, shocked that she hasn't had sex yet. I just assumed she wasn't a virgin. Then I scold myself. Maybe I'm just as shallow as everyone else she knew.

I hear stirring and casually put the journal under my pillow.

But it's just Trey, standing up in his crib. "ZiZi awake?" he asks with joyous surprise. "We can play?"

"Shh," I say, lifting my finger up. "It's early, Trey. Go back to bed."

I start pulling out the journal. I can probably get a few more minutes before my parents wake up.

"ZiZi," he whispers urgently.

"What?" I whisper back.

He lifts his arms in response. The gesture says it all: *Lift me, hold me, take off my diaper, start my day, I'm bored and being in this crib is torture.* "Use your words," I say, which is stupid since I actually want him to go back to sleep. But I'm so used to saying it now.

"Guppies," he whispers.

"Good job," I whisper back, with a thumbs-up.

When he sees this hasn't helped his cause, he yells out, "Guppies!"

And my mom wakes up.

———

It takes some effort to get away from my parents.

If they could put a tether on me, they would. My mom

166

won't let me "stay in the room all day" and has been urging me to see the online counselor at the Hang Out. I overheard her whispering to my dad about "depression." But I don't have depression. I'm sad about my friend, which I don't think is all that unreasonable.

Then I get a brilliant idea. "I was thinking maybe I'd go to the library today."

My mom and dad exchange glances. "Okay," my mom says.

When they're not looking, I shove the journal into my backpack, along with my copy of *Gatsby*. Then I peel off so they can witness me entering the library as my mom goes to yoga and my dad takes Trey to Guppies.

Luckily, the place is empty, most other passengers having more exciting places to be. The room is pretty nice, to be honest, with dark blue walls, wooden trim, a handsome pendulum clock on the wall, and a reasonable selection of books. I find myself checking out the YA section when I scold myself, *This is not why you're here, Izzy. Stick to the plan.* With a sigh, I gaze out the window, at the cloudy day, the gray line of the sea against a chalk-white sky.

Making myself comfortable by the window, I pull out the journal. The ticking clock keeps me company.

I have to tell Gram. I need that money for us, my mom and me. It isn't supposed to be for him anyway. He doesn't deserve it. He's in the casino all the time, and he's not even good at it! He just gambles it all away. He shouldn't be talking shit about my mom, when he's got an addiction too.

I read the words again, hardly believing them. But then I

167

consider it. Bob always seemed to be AWOL. And I saw him leaving the casino on more than one occasion.

Maybe that's why she hated them so much, because they were taking her money.

I start reading again.

BTW, more intel on the side job. I saw Diego whispering with Sergei, his Russian mob-bro. Here, she has drawn a pretty good representation of the scythe tattoo climbing up his neck. She never told me that she was a good artist. But then, I never got a chance to ask.

The clock tick-tocks across from me, the reflection of a bookshelf swaying on the brass pendulum.

He looked pissed as hell and yelled at Diego. "Keep her the fuck away from this. If she finds out about it, you're dead. Both of you."

And I'm like, what the fuck? Does her mean . . . me? What am I not supposed to find out?

I HAVE TO TALK TO DIEGO.

A sound startles me then, and I see my mom peeking in the doorway. I close the journal and grab a coffee-table book on birds to cover it. She sees me, and relief passes over her face. Her geeky daughter is indeed just wiling away the hours in the library.

She comes closer to the table and tilts her head to see the book. "Birds?" she asks with surprise. "That's a new one."

I shrug. "I saw different kinds at the beach."

"Oh," she says, but still doesn't look convinced. She knows me. I may be geeky, but not *that* geeky. "So anyway, I was thinking. If you're done in the library, maybe we could hit the spa?" she ventures. "Just us girls? I booked us both a hot stone massage just in case."

I would rather keep reading, but I don't have a good excuse. I can't exactly beg off to spend more time looking at birds. She would suss that one out for sure. "Sure," I say. "Why not?"

"Grab your stuff?" she asks, sounding chipper.

"Um . . ." I try to figure out if I can somehow slip the journal from under the bird book without her noticing. But I don't think so. And she'll get suspicious if I delay too much longer.

"Okay," I say, grabbing my backpack from my feet and praying no one puts away the bird book while we're gone.

My mom asks about birds on our way down there, and I stammer about how European starlings were introduced to America by a fan of Shakespeare, something I *am*, in fact, geeky enough to know. Then we get to the spa, an ultra-quiet, ivory-colored room that smells of vanilla. Enya plays softly in the background, and the ivory marble counter holds rows of overpriced lotions and hair products. A heavily Botoxed re-ceptionist with liberally applied copper eyeshadow takes our names and shows us to our lockers.

As we start taking off our clothes, I can't help but remember the spa day with Jade, and try not to picture her firecracker-red toenails, somewhere at the bottom of the ocean.

———

I try to enjoy the pampering—the mineral pool, the hot stone massage—but my brain is spinning.

What was Sergei talking about?

Is that what got Jade killed?

My mom, meanwhile, is the most relaxed I've seen her in years as we sit, dripping in our swimsuits in the steam room. An older woman covered with bleary tattoos, buzzed hair, and gargantuan breasts sits butt naked across from us. Every once and a while she moans in delight.

Mom keeps up a patter of conversation, wondering how Trey is doing, how lacrosse is going this year (not sure I'll even make varsity), whether I'll run for school council again (the answer is no, though I tell her maybe), and how Torts (our imperious cat, who still holds a grudge over her lawyer pun name) is faring with the sitter. My mom pries conversation out of me, discussing anything and everything—except Jade. I try to keep up the conversation, but my mind keeps dissecting the journal, which hopefully hasn't been taken.

After a while, the air grows stifling. Water beads on the tile walls, occasionally dripping onto us in an arrhythmic, disconcerting manner. A sheen of sweat covers me, though I'm not sure if it's actual sweat, steam, or the jasmine-infused lotion from the stone massage. Probably all three.

Finally, the woman stands, presenting me with equally gargantuan buttocks, and opens the door to leave. A pocket of cool air swishes in before we're swallowed up by the heat again. I rub my eyes, which sting with sweat and lotion. My breathing starts to feel labored, like that one year I had an asthma attack playing field hockey. The air feels thick and moist, too heavy to breathe.

"You okay?" my mom asks.

I nod. "I think I'd better get out, though."

As I stand, the room takes a carousel spin, and gray dots fill my vision. I put my palm on the wall, which slips.

"Whoa there," my mom says, and I feel her arms around me. A cool blast of air shivers through me as she opens the door. "Let's sit down for a minute," she instructs. "We need some water here," she barks out to an attendant.

A minute later, my mom hands me a glass of water, and a towel appears around me. As I drink the lemon-infused water, the gray dots start to dissipate. My breathing eases. I feel my muscles relax again. "You doing better, honey?" she asks.

I nod, trying not to move my head too much.

"Little dehydrated, probably." She gives my knee a pat. "Take your time. We can hit the locker room when you're ready."

"Okay," I say. I take another long drink of the water, and soon enough, am feeling nearly myself again. Or at least able to stand anyway. We get dressed in the locker room. My mom pays up at the front desk, the soft scent of vanilla filling the vestibule. The woman from the front desk hands us both a mini-bottle of water and a card from the spa with a hand-written note.

"'Come again soon,'" my mom reads. "Oh, isn't that nice?" She tucks it into her purse.

I hold my note, expecting the same. But my mouth goes chalk dry as I read the words.

If you don't stop, you're next.

twenty-eight

The note has been swept away, almost before I can register it. In its place comes the same note my mom has: a sugary-sweet *Come again soon!!* with a smiley face.

Aghast, I turn back to the receptionist, whose name tag says "Yvonne." But she appears unmoved, wearing the same professional, white-enamel smile that greeted us.

"Did you see that?" I ask stupidly. My knees have gone lax, and I'm clinging to the counter.

Yvonne makes a show of looking around. "What did you see, darling?" she asks in a French accent. Her face barely moves.

"The note," I say, the substitute note trembling in my fingers. "What happened to it? Did you throw it out?"

My mom turns to me with concern. "What note, honey? The come-again-soon one?"

"No . . . I . . ." I peer over the desk, but the paper has vanished.

Yvonne backs up with a nervous smile. "I don't know about a note . . . Did you . . . ?" She asks her coworker, who answers with a bored shrug.

"What did it say?" my mom asks, puzzled.

"It was a threat. . . ." My throat tightens with tears, and I swallow them back. " 'You'll be next.' It said I should stop or 'you'll be next.' "

Yvonne looks appropriately concerned. Maybe she didn't hand me the note? How did it get to me?

"Stop what?" Yvonne asks, tapping her long French-manicured nails on the counter as the soothing sounds of flutes and bells play in the background. The piped-in music just stirs up the turmoil in my head. Is she lying?

"Forget it," I mutter.

My mom pauses, her eyebrows scrunching. "Are you sure?"

"Yes," I say, frustrated. "Let's just go."

"Maybe you should have more water," my mom suggests as we walk out of the room, the soft spa music suddenly silent. "Your mind can play tricks on you when you're dehydrated."

"I saw it," I insist, spitting out the words. But my knees still feel spongy, my head light. Maybe she's right. Is it possible? That I'm seeing things?

"It's okay," my mom says, throwing her arm around me. "Maybe you should go back to the room. Get some rest."

But I saw it. I know I saw it.

If you don't stop, you're next.

Which means I'm definitely right. Jade didn't kill herself. I'm getting closer to the truth. And someone doesn't like it. But who? Who would even know that I doubted the suicide story? I suppose I've told just about everyone—the inspector, Bryce, Bob and Joanie. Or maybe someone has been spying on me and reporting back to Diego.

Maybe someone knows I have the journal. "I think I'll walk around the ship a little," I say. "Get some air."

My mom's face flashes worry. "I could come with you," she offers.

"You don't need to," I say, forcing a casual tone. "I might go to the Hang Out. See if Connor is there." Connor is a boy I just made up.

"Oh." Her nervous expression dissolves. *Just a boy; that I can handle.* "Okay," she says, "don't be back too late."

———

An elderly man in khakis and a blue shirt peruses the new fiction section of the library, opening a Patterson book. But when I get to my table, I notice it right away.

The bird book has vanished, along with the journal.

In a panic, I look over the desk, as if I would have missed it the first time. I stand up and look at all the seats in the table and the floor. Nothing. My heart clenching, I stand up and speed around the library, checking shelves, couch chairs, windowsills . . . but I don't see the purple paisley journal anywhere.

Someone must have taken it. Someone who didn't want me digging any deeper.

After gazing around the room in shock, I check my backpack. But of course it's not there.

"Did you lose something?" the older man asks, his book splayed open on his hand.

I swallow. "Um, my journal. Did you see it maybe? It was purple?"

174

He thinks about it for half a second, then gives an apologetic shrug. "Sorry," he says.

I run a shaky hand through my massage-oily hair, feeling like I might start crying. I should have put it in my backpack. I could have snuck it in there in time.

"You could ask the lost and found, dear," he says in a grandfatherly way, probably seeing my crushed expression. "It can't have gone far."

What was the last thing she wrote? *I have to talk to Diego.*

Maybe he knows something about her disappearance. Or more likely, he's involved.

If you don't stop, you're next.

I need to get that journal.

———

At the front desk, I bite my nails waiting for the receptionist to check the lost and found. To calm my panicking mind, I focus on the wall in the back office, reading the notices. There's a huge schematic of this ship, too. I think I've been on every deck except for the lower decks. I squint to see the odd names—poop deck, boiler deck, bridge deck, with further descriptions written within each deck. Crew bunks . . . safety gear . . . storage. The receptionist returns, and I stop looking, though I'm sure a picture of the ship isn't a secret. "Nope, honey, sorry," she says. A bobby pin shines in her soft updo. "You lost it today?"

I nod, not trusting myself to speak.

"Hm," she says. "Maybe someone took it along with the bird book, not noticing it. Do you think that could be?"

I lick my lips. "It's possible," I admit. But it might be more sinister. And then it hits me. The journal was hidden under the book, not just lying around for all to see. So who would have even known it was under there? Maybe someone *is* spying on me.

"Would you like us to call you if we find it?" the receptionist asks, her expression soft and kind. She checks her computer. "I have your room number right here—"

"No, no," I break in. "I'll check back." I don't want my parents finding out if she leaves a message in the room.

"Sure thing," she answers as a woman steps up after me, asking about more paper for the computer room printer.

My brain feels spacey as I walk away.

If you don't stop, you're next.

CHAPTER

twenty-nine

The track smells faintly of rubber. I run laps, just to do something with my body and keep my brain from flying into madness. I went back to the library, but of course the journal wasn't there. I tried Jade's room, but the key didn't work anymore—not shocking. And why would it be in there anyway?

I don't know who to tell or what to do.

I don't know what Sergei was warning Diego about, but if they think I know, then I'm dead too. I keep running, my breath raspy as the heat bakes my scalp, my earbuds sweaty in my ears. My thin coverup smells like a mixture of algae-infused-lavender oil and sweat from the massage, which feels like days instead of hours ago.

Who sent that note?

Her aunt and uncle? Bryce? Diego?

I could call the inspector, but he seemed more than happy to latch on to the suicide story, so the passengers could go home and the police could leave already. And he seemed to be hiding something. Maybe he's in on it, whatever it is. *He* could have gotten someone to give me the note.

"On your left," a jogger says, sending my heart jumping.

I shift out of the way as the jogger runs ahead into the underbelly of the ship. Before long, the track brings me into the same dark, musty area. A metallic sound bangs out in the hot, stuffy air. *Bang, bang,* like the pipes want to explode. I emerge into the sunlight again and keep running.

Who sent me the note?

Footsteps clomp behind me, and I move over to see Bryce pass me. He jogs shirtless, sweat beading on his chest, and nods at me, but he doesn't bother to stop running. I don't mind. We have nothing to say to each other. I think about what Jade said, about the anger in his eyes, and how he snapped at that kid in the hot tub, as he disappears around the bend.

Then I catch sight of someone below. A figure striding around in all white, large and in charge. Slipping my earbuds out, I can hear his loud Australian accent. "Having fun out there? Excellent. Good to see. Cracking good time."

He might be kind of phony and totally clueless, but if anyone can help me with a problem on the ship, it would be the captain.

———

"Excuse me," I say, still short of breath from racing down to the pool deck. The captain turns around, breaking into a smile.

"Izzy," he says with genuine pleasure, as if we hadn't seen each other in years. "Tell me, my dear. What can I do you for?"

I brush a piece of hair from my forehead, trying to think of where to start. The steel drums are playing Britney Spears, and I can hardly concentrate.

When he sees me struggling, he motions to a chair and we sit at a little table between the Breakaway Café and the pool. A server with a hamburger and fries passes us, and the captain rubs his hands together. "Have to get me one of those, huh?" He chuckles. "People forget that the captains need food too. I mean—"

"I think Jade was killed," I say, the words rushing out.

He stares at me, his ginger eyebrows furrowed in surprise. His sunny disposition has faded. "Why do you say that, Izzy?" A warm breeze blows over us, stirring up the scent of lavender from my lotion. "I mean, she sent you that text, right?"

"Right," I admit. "But I don't think she sent it. I think someone just wanted us to *think* that."

"Okay," he says evenly. I can see what he's thinking. *Is she crazy? Just girl drama?*

"She had money . . . a lot of money . . . and I think someone killed her for it." I get the words out before I lose my nerve.

"I didn't hear about any money," he says calmly, interlacing his fingers. "I would think the inspector would have mentioned it if there were."

I don't tell him my doubts about the inspector, because then he'll definitely write me off as delusional. "Jade talked about it," I say, not mentioning the journal for now. "I think someone from the casino was threatening her. Over drugs or something."

"Drugs?" he asks, appearing perturbed for the first time. "We don't have any drugs on this ship."

You might want to investigate that further, I think.

Frowning, he assesses me again. "Well, if you know

179

something, then I need to know about it. I need names. And I'll need to speak with the inspector again."

I don't answer right away, because what if I'm wrong?

"Do you have a name, Izzy?" he asks, pressing me. His blue eyes stay fixed on me, dead serious.

Uncomfortable, I clear my throat as a big splash reverberates from the pool. "I don't want to get them in trouble."

He gives me a smile of encouragement. "Well, if they're innocent, they won't be. Right?" He pulls a little pad out of his chest pocket.

"Um . . ." I twiddle my fingers. "Diego . . . I don't know his last name. He does the blackjack table at the casino." The captain nods, jotting something and underlining it. "And Sergei. He's—"

"Oh," he says, with an eyeroll. "Everybody knows Sergei." Another loud splash sounds out, followed by parental scolding. He looks up from his pad. "Anyone else?"

I shake my head. "I don't think so."

"Okay," he says, pocketing the notebook. "I will absolutely be looking into this. Thank you, Isabel. Thank you very much." He starts to stand up.

"And—" I break in. "Someone gave me a note."

With clear reluctance, he sits back down. "What's this about, then?" he asks, his tone brimming with polite impatience.

"Nothing," I say. "It's no big deal."

"Great," he says, booming and cheerful again. "I'll look into your concern, Isabel. I run a clean ship. And I take great pride in that," he adds with a forceful nod. "If someone is interfering with that, I will find out."

CHAPTER

thirty

A cruise chat message comes in as we're getting ready for dinner. After showering all the massage crap off, I'm putting on some of my only remaining clean clothes when it comes. It's from the receptionist.

Found your journal! 💋

Without meaning to, I jump into the air. An actual jump for joy.

"What's that about?" my mom asks, smiling at my good mood, and rakes gel into her hair.

I grab the opportunity. "Um, there's a Hang Out pizza party. So . . . do you mind if I skip—"

"Of course, of course," my mom says with an expansive hand gesture. My dad opens the bathroom, and steam flows out. "Don't you worry about it. You go have fun."

As she turns to talk to my dad, I leave the room and book down to guest services. The receptionist is there.

"Here you go," she says, handing it to me with a flourish.

"Thank you, thank you," I say. Then I pause. "Do . . . do you know who had it?"

"Oh," she says, thinking. She straightens the *Crown Jewel*

button on her lapel. "The librarian found it. Someone took it out with another book, I guess."

I hug it to my chest. "Thanks again," I say, amazed that I had an ounce of good luck today. And I should have a solid hour to read the book before my parents come back from dinner.

In bright spirits, I walk along the outside of the ship, heading back to the room. In the darkening night, I spy an orange spark of light up ahead. Walking toward the light, I catch a whiff of the dirty smell of cigarettes, and the spark lights up a handsome face.

Diego.

———

Before I know it, I am leaning on the rail next to him. "Hi," I say.

He regards me with a flicker of displeasure, then turns back to the ocean. A warm breeze flaps the cigarette between his lips. Without looking at me, he removes a pack of cigarettes from his breast pocket, the box half empty and sunken in. He slips a cigarette from the pack with a silky swish. "You want one?"

I shake my head.

With a shrug, he slots the cigarette back in, pocketing the pack again. "You here about Jade?"

I nod. "Did you hear about the text?" I ask, holding on to the railing.

"Yeah, everyone did." We're silent for a moment. I pick

out the stars of the Big Dipper, which is about the limit of my astronomical knowledge.

"Did she say anything to you?" I ask, turning to him. "That would make you think she would do that?"

He blows out a cone of smoke, which disappears in the wind. "Nope."

"Were you guys . . . going out or something?" I ask, embarrassed at the juvenile wording.

After sucking on the cigarette, he glances at me with uncertainty. "Why, what did she say?"

I pause. "That you were," I say, though she didn't exactly.

"Then she's a liar," he says, the words heated. He darts his cigarette into the ocean. "We barely did anything."

Barely? She's *sixteen* years old.

"Anyway, it doesn't really matter now, does it?" he snarls. "She offed herself."

I swallow, moving a step away. "And you knew nothing about it?"

"Why would I know anything about it?" he asks. "Weren't you two supposed to be besties or whatever? You're the one who got the text."

"I'm not sure she even did it, though," I say with a forced bravado. "I think somebody pushed her and just wants us to think it's suicide." I pause to let the words settle.

Diego takes a step toward me, his face an inch away from mine. "I think you should be careful. Very, very careful about what you say." I can still smell the smoke on his breath. "And you shouldn't be poking your nose where it doesn't belong."

I told Bob. I told them that I knew about the gambling and was telling Gram.

Man went BALLISTIC. Never seen him like that. Screaming, calling me a bitch, fucking brat. Aunt Joanie actually had to hold him back. "You do that," he said. "And you'll be sorry."

I told him I didn't care. I'm gonna live with Gram.

Fuck him. He'll be the one who's sorry when Gram cuts him off.

With a whir, the door swings open. "Hi!" I say, too brightly. "You're back early."

"Yeah," Mom says, and I get why when my dad lugs a hollering Trey into the room. "Someone's having a little tantrum." My mom sighs and plops onto her bed, lying down with her arms to the side like a dead person. "How was the pizza?" she asks.

"Oh," I say, remembering my lie just in time. "It was fine." My brain spins. I need to keep reading. I need to figure out what happened with her uncle.

Trey hiccups. "I think it's gonna be an early night for all of us," Mom says.

I fake a yawn. "Yeah, me too. I'm exhausted."

After a while, Trey cries himself to sleep, and my parents read for almost an hour while I pretend to watch soccer. Finally, they turn the television and the lights off.

I can still hear people in the hallway. Women laughing, men drunkenly calling to one another. Doors opening and shutting, couples bickering. I wait and wait, until my dad starts snoring and my mom's breathing evens. Then, with my phone light on under the sheets, I keep reading, turning the pages as slowly as I can.

Hung out with Diego in his room. Shared a joint. Out of nowhere he starts telling me about this thing with him and Sergei. Like he was guilty and needed to tell someone. Now I know how he could afford that necklace. He told me about his side deal.

They're smuggling drugs onto the ship.

I gasp out loud, and my mom murmurs in her sleep, so I turn the light off and wait again. When she seems settled again, I turn the light back on.

Not just pot either, like, heroin, cocaine, and meth and all that. He said they bring it on food crates in Bermuda, and Diego sells it in NYC when they dock. Sergei just beats people up I guess. Diego started bragging, said they make millions.

So I figured out a way I could get an apartment with my mom. I don't even need my uncle's stupid money.

I take a deep breath, not realizing that I was holding it.

I told him I want 10K to keep his secret.

Diego looked pissed, but why not?? If he's making millions, 10K is nothing.

Out of nowhere, Trey screams. I turn the light off as my mom pops out of her bed to go over to him. "Shh . . . it's okay."

"Monsters," he cries. "I saw monsters."

So she was blackmailing him, then.

I lie there, my hands still gripping the journal, and pretend to be asleep.

CHAPTER

thirty-one

DAY 13

Final Day at Sea

The next day, I decide to show the captain the journal. He wanted evidence, and this seems pretty ironclad. And even if he wants to keep it, I have read the whole thing. There's nothing more to discover.

But the problem is that I can't find the captain. Mr. Friendly, who always seems to be everywhere, is nowhere to be found. I roam around the ship with my backpack banging against me, the journal waiting inside like a bomb ready to detonate. The guard at the officers' quarters politely tells me he's not there, and I can't get in without a security pass anyway. I walk by the Bon Voyage Theater but figure he's probably not catching a matinee of *Honey, I Shrunk the Kids*.

I don't see him until dinner that evening, after I've already stashed the journal in our room in the back of the highest shelf in the closet.

Tonight's theme, Prom Night, is stupider than most. My dad wears a tuxedo with a shocking-pink cummerbund, and my mom, a black satiny dress. Trey has a clip-on tie, which already has mucus on it from a cold that he got from the Guppies. I'm wearing a half-decent coral dress that my mom bought me for the cruise. So, at least, I didn't have to waste my own money on it.

Trey plays with his mac and cheese while my dad eats a lobster, which is more shell than meat. My mom has yet another headache, and I can't eat a thing.

I hear footsteps behind me and glance up to see the captain. He leans back on his heels grinning. "Having a fun prom night?" he asks.

Trey answers with a loud, green, mucous-y sneeze.

"Oh," he says, looking horrified. "Someone's got a cold, huh?"

"Yeah," my mom says with a pained smile.

"I was thinking of the captain's tour tonight," he says. "But . . . maybe tomorrow would be better." I'm guessing he doesn't want sneeze droplets everywhere.

"That sounds good," my dad says with a yearning glance at the rest of his lobster.

The captain gets the signal and pats my dad on the back. "Excellent. So, we'll reach out tomorrow for the tour."

Trey releases another hellacious sneeze.

"Do you mind?" my mom asks, pointing to my soda. I push it over to her, since I haven't even had a sip yet.

"This stupid headache," she gripes. She takes a long gulp, then passes it back to me.

But considering the germs floating around this family, I decide to forego the drink. "All yours," I say, pushing it back.

"Thanks," she says with a grateful nod and takes another sip. "The caffeine will kick in soon, I'm sure."

The ship takes a lurch, and a collective moan rolls across the room, followed by nervous laughter, like when a plane takes a roller-coaster drop and all the passengers pretend everything is fine, just fine.

In fact, this whole evening feels that way to me. As if this is a normal trip without a dead girl, as if dressing up means anything. Now it's dessert time, and the waitstaff start jogging around with bananas Foster to the tune of "Celebration." My father leans back in his chair with a genuine smile, enjoying the spectacle. Trey also seems entranced by the fiery plates, rising above the sedation of cold medicine. The whole boat tilts again, and the servers gamely recover their footing, though I'm wondering if open fire is such a good idea on a raging sea.

Out of nowhere, my mom bursts into a loud laugh.

"What?" I ask, wondering if she's finding the whole facade ridiculous too, but she looks weird. Flushed and glassy-eyed.

She shakes her head. "Nothing." She keeps shaking her head, though, as if she can't stop shaking it.

My dad gives her a good-natured smile. "I think she had a little too much to drink at the whiskey tasting."

But she didn't even seem tipsy at the start of the dinner.

"Celebration . . . ," the staff sings, doing a sort of jig and passing out dishes. The whole thing is giving me a headache too. My dad taps his hand to the rhythm of the song,

bouncing the whole table. I check on my mom again, who seems to be reaching out for something. "Mom?" I ask.

"I'll get it," she mumbles, snatching at something in the air. "Don't worry." She gives me a quick smile of reassurance.

"Get what?" I ask, searching the air for a fly or something.

Trey drums his spoon on the table in time with the music, and my dad smiles at him.

My mom takes another swipe at the air. "I almost got it that time," she says. Then she gives me a weird smile. Her pupils are blown out, and her eyes look almost black.

"Dad," I say.

He turns to me with a thrilled look. "It's terrific, isn't it?"

"Fire," Trey says. A whoosh of the heat touches my face, and then the flame is quickly doused, creating a charred, nauseating smell.

"Dad," I repeat, with urgency this time. "There's something wrong with Mom." My dad turns to see what I'm talking about.

"Got it!" my mom says, grabbing at something invisible.

"Honey?" my dad asks, alarm flashing in his eyes.

"I've got it, Ted," she answers with a heartfelt smile. Then she falls right over, her face smacking the table.

CHAPTER
thirty-two

With an IV in her arm, Mom comes to in the infirmary, a cramped room on the periphery of the ship. The room appears to be an afterthought, barely big enough to fit the patient, doctor, and family, with some funky carpet stains and scuffs on the wall. Mom lies on a medical bed, which carries a strong resemblance to my cot, while our whole family crowds her. Trey shifts his sleepy head on my father's shoulder.

"Anticholinergic toxicity," the doctor says with a buoyant smile, as if he just answered a *Jeopardy!* question. He wears a white coat over shorts and a T-shirt, his hair a grizzled salt and pepper. His little rectangular badge reads "Dr. Wang."

"Excuse me?" my mom asks. She still appears flushed, in a daze. The doctor wheels over to her in his squeaky chair. I notice a Kermit the Frog tattoo on his forearm and try to imagine the life decision that led to that. I don't think I would trust this guy with Torts.

"Have you been on the patch? For seasickness?" he asks. He's talking about the motion-sickness patch thingy that I ditched after feeling drowsy the whole first day.

"Yes," she answers, her eyebrows scrunched in thought. "But not for a couple of days."

"No?" he asks, with a quizzical eyebrow. "How about Benadryl?"

"I'm not on Benadryl," she says, unsuccessfully trying to sit up. Her arms shake with the effort.

"We gave Trey some for his cold," my dad says, whispering so as not to wake my brother. He sways lightly side to side in a lulling motion. "Maybe it got mixed up in your meds somehow?"

"Maybe . . . ," my mom says.

"I'm going with the patch," Dr. Wang says, as if this were a horse race. *Yeah, I'll put a hundred down on patch.* He picks up a poppy-seed bagel from his desk and takes a bite. "Probably got a bit too much in your system and overdosed. Scopolamine toxicity," he says, between bites. "We see it all the time."

"But I haven't worn one in days," my mom argues.

He swallows. "Did one break open maybe? Could you have ingested it by accident?" he asks. "Stranger things have happened."

"I don't think so," she says, though her tone is less certain.

Dr. Wang zigzags his chair back to his computer. "We do see it a lot here, though. People going a little crazy with the anticholinergic meds." He gives a what-can-ya-do shrug. *You can't stop people going crazy with those anticholinergic meds!* "Anyway, your EKG looks fine. So after we're done with the bag"—he points to the pouch on the IV pole—"it's up to you. You can stay or go."

"Go," my mom says, the word shooting out of her mouth. She smiles, softening her obvious desire to get the hell out of there. "I mean, I know where you are if there's a problem."

"Yup," he says, sounding not offended in the least. "Like I said, your call. Just got to take out that IV, print up your discharge summary, and vamoose—you're good to go."

My dad clears his throat. "So, should I take him back?" He tilts his head at Trey.

"Definitely," my mom says. "Go. I won't be long." She meets my eyes. Her pupils still look big, but not alarmingly so. "You go too, honey," she says. "I'm fine."

I glance at my dad. "I'll stay," I say. "Since it won't be long."

He nods with a tired smile as Dr. Wang taps on the keyboard, intermittently chomping on his bagel. I hold my mom's hand, which feels dry and small. She gives mine a squeeze, closing her eyes. For a minute, I have the unsettling feeling that I'm the mom, and she's the child. I wonder if this is how Jade felt with her mom. The thought makes me want to cry.

"I just don't know how I could have gotten it," my mom says, rubbing her eyes. "I mean, it's not like I go around eating patches or something."

That's when it hits me. "Ingesting them," I say.

"Makes no sense, right?" my mom comments, a yawn poking through.

Ingesting them doesn't just mean eating them. It could also mean drinking them. And what's an easy way to get rid

192

of someone on a ship, without anyone suspecting? If this kind of diagnosis is "routine" around here, no one would question if someone accidentally died of it. It would be frighteningly easy to empty a couple of patches into someone's soda.

The soda that I was supposed to drink.

CHAPTER
thirty-three

"I mean it, Mom," I say, the words spilling out after the doctor leaves the room. "First the note, now this. You've got to believe me."

"Honey," my mom says, clasping her hands together, "I know this has been very difficult. But whatever happened, I can assure you, no one was trying to kill me."

"That's the thing," I say in a loud whisper, though I'm unsure why I'm whispering. Surely no one has bugged the doctor's office.

Now I am really going crazy.

"It's not you," I say, still whispering. "They were trying to poison *me*."

"Honey," she repeats, this time sternly, in a pull-it-together voice. "You're starting to scare me."

"Good," I say, though it comes out in a giddy half shriek. "We should be scared. They killed Jade, and now they want to kill me."

With strong effort, my mom sits up on one elbow. "Listen. This cruise has been tough on everyone. And I know you've had a bit of a shock here. You more than anyone, but—"

"No, no, no!" I say, gripping her blanket. "I know it sounds weird and crazy. I know that. But I'm not delusional."

She lifts herself an inch higher, a sigh escaping. "I'm not saying *delusional* exactly, it's just—"

"No," I shout-whisper, leaning my elbows on her cot. My brain feels like it's on fire, and no one will listen to me. "Please."

"Izzy," she says, putting her hand on my arm. "You really need to calm down. Okay? There's nothing I can do about this right now. When we get home, which is soon, I can get you in touch with a friend. She's an excellent psychiatrist. And a trauma specialist."

"Jesus, Mom." Pushing away from her bed, I stand up and start pacing the little room. "I don't need a psychiatrist."

"There's no shame in seeing a psychiatrist," she says, her eyes following me.

"I know that," I say, huffing. "Miranda's been seeing a psychiatrist since she's been, like, two. Believe me, in my school, it's weird if you *don't* see a psychiatrist." I drop down to the chair again, my head falling into my hands.

"Then what's the problem?" she asks tenderly.

I perch on the edge of the chair, feeling like I might just launch out of it. "The problem is no one believes me!"

"You know what?" she asks. Slowly, she pulls herself to a sitting posture. "Why don't you go back to the room?" She sounds short of breath with the effort of sitting up. "Get some sleep, okay? It's been a long day, with the spa and then my little episode."

"A little episode?" I screech. "Mom, you were freaking poisoned."

The door opens then, the doctor striding in with a sheet of paper in hand. "Voilà," he says, handing her the paper with a flourish. "All set. Remember, if you need me, the doctor is in."

———

It's about two-thirty in the morning by the time we get back to the room.

We make slow progress, my mom gripping my arm with one hand and the railing with the other. But she seems to gain strength as we near the room. Hopefully the poison is finally exiting her system. She flops into bed with my dad, and by the time I have my pj's on, she's fast asleep. Lying on the cot, I close my eyes and try to do the same.

But my brain keeps screaming at me.

Someone tried to kill you!

I could tell the inspector. But he thinks I'm crazy too. Caleb and Bryce are completely unhelpful. I wish I could call Miranda, but that's impossible.

I could tell Jade.

This fragment of thought swerves into my head once again before I can even filter it. The only person who might understand me right now is dead. Tears creep into my eyes, and I close them again, rolling over to sleep.

My heart ping-pongs in my chest, knocking against my sternum. I open my eyes to blackness and close them again, but then have the sudden sensation of falling backward. Maybe this was how Jade felt when she fell overboard. The ocean feels too insubstantial, as if it might not hold us up. All at once, it seems impossible that water could possibly hold a ship. My heart starts bouncing again, and my breath goes short.

I sit up.

My eyes darting around the room, I fight the panic surging through me.

Almost unconsciously, I take deep breaths, calming my banging heart, the way our health teacher taught us. After a few more breaths, my heart slows to a normal rhythm. My brain understands that the walls are just the walls, a cocoon protecting me, not a cage closing in on me. The water is dense, stronger than the wood or steel on this boat.

I am safe.

I keep repeating this in my head. *I am safe. I am safe. I am safe.*

But then the silence in the room strikes me. Trey might be on cold meds, but he is never this quiet. And if they tried to kill me, they might try to kill him too.

Leaping off the cot, I rush over to his crib. He lies there, completely still, his chest not moving.

My hand shaking, I put my palm on his chest.

And . . . he's breathing. He's breathing just fine.

Exhaling with relief, I stagger back to my cot. Maybe everyone's right. I really am going crazy.

This time when I close my eyes, I fall asleep.

CHAPTER

thirty-four

When I finally wake up, the room is still silent, my mom still asleep. Quietly, I get up and see a note propped up on the bureau.

Working out. Trey is with Guppies. Come get me if you need me.

XO,

Dad

I check on my mom, still a little flushed from the poisoning. The memory of last night sinks my stomach. Images flit through my head like a movie reel—my mom grabbing at imaginary flies, lying in a cot with an IV in her arm, the doctor's Kermit the Frog tattoo, Trey so quiet and . . . My brain starts spooling into a panic again, and I take deep breaths, trying to short-circuit the flood of fear.

After a final exhale, my heart rate lowers, and my breathing evens.

I am safe. The mantra grounds me. *I am safe. I am safe.*

But then another voice worms into my head. *No, you are not safe.*

They threatened you. They tried to poison you.

You are not at all safe.

I throw some clothes on, to quiet the skirmish in my brain.

I have to do something. I can't just sit here fighting off panic attacks. I don't know who's behind this, but I need to find out.

———

In the blinking casino lights, I catch Diego's eye right away, but he pretends not to see me. He thwaps cards on the table for two passengers. They look like new college graduates, both wearing Penn State swag and concentrating on their cards. "What did you do to her?" I demand.

Everyone at the table turns to look at me, and I realize maybe that was a little direct.

"Didn't do anything to her," he grunts at me, treating me like an annoying kid sister.

I inch closer to the blackjack table. "She was blackmailing you," I say in a low voice. His upper lip twitches for just a second, a hint of a wince.

"You're nuts," he says, annoyed.

But I saw the twitch. He's not much of a poker player.

"Hit," one of the Penn State guys says. Diego delivers a card.

"You gave her the ketamine, and she found out you were dealing drugs," I say, still in a quiet voice.

"Nope," he says at a normal volume.

"Hit," the player says again, and gets another card. From the corner of the room, Sergei gives Diego a questioning look, and he shakes his head with a half smirk. *Nah. I can handle this one.*

"Stay," the other player says, holding a hand up.

"You wanted the money back," I say, louder this time. "Didn't want people to know you were dealing."

199

He gives me a smooth smile. "Everyone knows I'm a dealer, right, guys?"

They chuckle, happy to be in on the joke as part of the boys club.

"Bust," one of them says with a dejected slump. He pushes his chips to Diego.

"I'm going to find out what happened to Jade," I warn. "You can threaten me all you want, but I'm going to do it. I'm not going to stop, not ever. . . ."

Diego throws me a bemused look. "Threaten you? Who's threatening you. Kid, I don't care about you enough to threaten you."

I examine his face. No twitches this time. He actually seems like he doesn't know what I'm talking about. Two men in tight shirts and preppy Bermudas stroll over. "You open?" one of them asks.

"Have a seat," Diego answers, all smiles again.

"Listen," I say, though he has clearly checked out of the conversation. "I told the captain and—"

He honks out a laugh, smoothing the polished wood with his hand. "Oh, no," he says. He puts on a faux-frightened expression. "She told the *captain*."

Before I can say anything else, Sergei turns up by my side. He gives me a slimy smile. "I'm very sorry, young lady. You must be twenty-one to be in the casino alone. I must ask you to leave now."

My face flames. "Fine," I say. "I'm going." Then I point right at Diego. "I know what you did. I know it."

"Time to go," Sergei says with ice in his voice. "Now."

On the heels of that resounding failure, I decide to take a break from my inept investigation. Lying on a beach chair, I pick up an unclaimed *Vogue* magazine, the pages puffy from dampness. But I can barely read a word.

Someone tried to poison you.

If you don't stop, you're next.

I slap the magazine shut, trying to shut down my brain too. I gaze up at the sky, a deep blue with white popcorn clouds. It's a jarring juxtaposition, the beauty of this setting against the ugliness of Jade's disappearance. A paradise sky and a bloody sleeve. It seems impossible this day could be so lackadaisical, full of sunning and fashion magazines, when there's a murderer out there who killed Jade and is now trying to kill me.

I'm still staring at the sky when I hear a familiar happy chirping. I shield my eyes to block the sun and see Trey standing near the railing. But he's not with his Guppy group.

As I climb out of my chair, Trey giggles and points to the railing. One of the staff members, who looks about twenty, bends down to his level, smiling and talking. He puts his arm around his shoulders and points to something way off in the distance. Maybe they've seen a dolphin, or a whale even. But I don't trust anyone right now, so I stand up to check it out. My flip-flops thwack as I meet up with them. The man has a crisp white shirt without a name tag and a glossy, well-manicured goatee.

"Hey," I say, and Trey's face lights up. "What's up?"

"Mermaids!" Trey says, bopping up and down with excitement.

"Oh," I say, with a beat of relief. Obviously I'm a bit paranoid right now. The guy's just telling Trey mermaid stories.

"If you fall, they catch you," Trey adds, nodding at the man.

I let out a nervous laugh and automatically move closer to Trey. "What do you mean they catch you?"

Trey tiptoes for a better look through the rails. "People fall off. Mermaids catch you."

My body goes rigid as the man and I stare at each other. "No, Trey. Mermaids aren't real," I say.

"It doesn't hurt. They catch you!" He throws up his arms to demonstrate.

I drop to a squat and meet his gaze. "Listen to me, Trey. If you fall off the ship, you die. Nobody catches you. Mermaids aren't real."

His face crumples at my unusually stern tone. "He told me," he says, pointing up to put the blame on the man. I shoot the crew member a look, but his expression remains impassive.

In shock, I grab Trey's hand tightly, pulling him away from the all-too-tempting railing. "Come on, Trey," I say. "Let's get you back to the Guppies." Before I turn around, I hear the crewman's voice.

"He's right," the man says, smoothing his goatee. "Kids need to be careful." He holds my eyes for a second, then gives me a cold smile. "Or they can have accidents too."

CHAPTER
thirty-five

"I'm sure that's not what he meant," my mom says in a scolding tone after I tell her what happened. I am pacing our stateroom before dinner. She has fully recovered and reverted to being annoying again.

"Is there a theme tonight, hon?" my dad calls out from the bathroom.

"No, just regular," she calls back. "Which is good because I have no clean clothes."

"Mom," I say, stopping and grabbing her arm. "I'm not kidding. You should see the way he said it. It was . . . creepy. Like it was a threat."

"Said be careful," Trey says with a serious head wag, standing there naked except for his big boy underpants.

"That's right," my mom emphasizes with a finger point while picking out elastic-waist jeans. "You do have to be careful."

"Mermaids *are* real," Trey adds, a direct reproach to my stern denial.

"That's right," my mom agrees again. "We read that book about mermaids, remember?"

"You don't understand," I say, pacing again, wanting to cry with frustration. "They poisoned you when they meant to poison me. And now they're threatening Trey."

Her look of annoyance morphs into concern. "Honey," she says quietly. Here she goes, the PTSD thing again. "I'm worried about your mental health. Really."

"Mom," I say urgently.

"It's not your fault," she assures me. "Everyone responds differently to stress. And with PTSD."

"I don't have freaking PTSD!" I yell, jumping up and down in frustration, which makes me look like I have PTSD. My father exits the bathroom and gives me a worried look.

"Wait a second," I say. "Let me show you something." I run to the closet, pushing my lacrosse stick out of the way and grunting to reach the top, where I stashed the journal. Smoothing the top shelf with my hand, I feel nothing. "What the . . . ?"

"Here," my dad says. "Let me check." He scoots next to me. "Make way for the tall guy," he says, with a smile. Then he takes a peek. "Nothing up there, hon."

"No?" I ask, my voice trembling. "Nothing? Are you sure?"

"Yup," he says, patting the wood. "Clean as a whistle."

"Oh my God," I say, sinking into the cot.

"What?" my mom asks, grabbing my shoulder. "What's going on, Izzy?"

"Nothing," I say, popping up from the bed.

I have to find the man with the goatee.

thirty-six

In the hub by the elevators, unbelievably, I see him.

But just as quickly as I spot him, he disappears, slithering into a crowd. I bolt after him, but lose him right away. I dip my head into the kitchen but don't see him there. I guess on a right turn through the Pineapple Bar but still don't catch him. Ditto the YOLO Club and the Blue Velvet Lounge. Staff pop up everywhere, of course, a dizzying array of white shirts and black vests, but he's a needle in a haystack.

He might not even be involved in her death. Someone could have easily bribed him. Flash a hundred dollars at someone, and they might take a toddler to the railing and make up stories about mermaids and jumping.

But even so, if I can find him, maybe he can give me information.

I sweep through every nook and cranny on the cruise ship. The pool deck, bingo in the deck room, the Bon Voyage Theater, the Lizard Lounge, the piano bar, the mall shops, the 24-7 Caffeine Fix. I even run through the casino, careful to avoid Sergei.

The search takes me more than an hour, and by the end

I'm ragged, sweating, and empty-handed. I end up right back in the hub where I first saw him. But I'm no closer to him. It's easy to hide in a floating city, especially if you know the place inside and out.

I'm about to give up when, astonishingly, there he is again. Slipping out of an employee-only doorway, his lithe form strides ahead of me.

"Hey," I say, belting out the word.

The man speeds up, and so do I, practically running. "Hey," I call out again, and he still doesn't turn around. Jogging, I finally catch up to him, and grab him by the shoulder, twisting him around. "Hey!" I yell.

But it's not him.

"Excuse me?" the staff member says nervously. "Can I help you?"

Mortified, I take a step back. "I'm sorry. No, I'm fine. I . . . I thought you were someone else."

"Okay," he says, with a forgiving nod, and goes on his way again.

I'm standing there in shock when my mom passes by.

She stops, putting her arm on my shoulder. "You okay?" she asks, coming closer. "You look like you just saw a ghost."

"No," I murmur. Not a ghost. A wily, evil man with a goatee.

"Okay," she says, her tone weighted with worry. "Why don't we get some dinner?"

———

After dessert, the captain keeps his word on the quarters grand tour for tonight.

"You ready, buddy?" the captain asks Trey as we stand outside the room. Trey nods excitedly, like one of those cymbal-clapping monkeys. The captain pushes the door open with a flourish, revealing all the wonders that lie inside. He takes a seat in a wooden director's chair, with a panel of buttons beneath him. The ship's steering wheel is enormous, made of fine shiny wood and a brass ring in the center. It looks more ornamental than functional.

Trey leaps into the room and starts hopping all over, immediately pushing buttons. The double brownie sundae at dinner probably didn't help. "Whoa there, son," the captain says with a big fake grin.

"Trey," my mom scolds, embarrassed.

"That's okay. Just trying to keep things safe," the captain says, smiling at Trey as if he actually wants to smack him.

"Yeah, we don't want to hit any icebergs or anything," my dad jokes. The captain smiles at my dad as if he wants to smack him too.

"Pretty cool, huh?" one of the crew members says. He's also in all white, but with less decorations on his uniform, so probably an underling of some sort. His name tag says "Sven." Trey bops over to Sven, and the captain appears happy to be relieved of Trey-watch.

"Did you know," Sven asks, "that more historical artifacts lie in the bottom of the ocean than in all of the museums in the world?" My mom covers a yawn, hiding a bored expression, as Sven excitedly discusses some of his bigger finds. My dad asks about everything possible—tides, different weather patterns, storm indicators, radar. I might die of boredom.

Trey probably feels the same and reaches to hit a giant red button on the control panel. Sven catches his hand just in time. "Oh no, my friend, we don't want to do that."

"Why?" Trey asks.

"Because," the captain says, walking over, "That is a *big* SOS button. And that means a lot of people will hop on our ship and be very unhappy with us if we pushed it just for fun."

"S-O . . . ?" Trey asks, still eyeing the very tempting button.

"SOS," my dad whispers to him. "Save Our Ship."

Trey does not comprehend.

"It's getting late," my mom offers, to the relief of everyone.

My father nods, bouncing on his toes. "I just had one more question about—"

"Ted," my mom says in a sweet tone that says *we are leaving right now.* We all gather around my mom, heading toward the exit, including my disappointed father.

"Izzy," the captain says as we leave, just above a whisper. "I looked into your concerns. Did a thorough search. Nothing to worry about." He puts his arm around my shoulders.

"Thanks," I say. But jeez, the man is completely clueless.

———

Back in our room, Trey lies in his crib, asleep before my mom finishes putting on his pajamas. My dad brushes his teeth in the bathroom.

"I thought we'd never get out of there," my mom complains, pulling her arms through the sleeves of her nightshirt.

"I thought it was pretty cool," my dad says, his mouth full of toothpaste foam.

"Yeah, I could tell," she says, sliding under her sheets with a contented sigh. She grabs her hardcover library book with a woman lying on the beach on the cover, while my dad does this gross ten-minute-long gargle-and-spit thing.

Out of nowhere, my phone pings.

"Who's that?" my mom asks, pushing her reading glasses lower on her nose.

"Miranda, probably," I say, since she's the only one who texts me anymore. She's probably asking me about Luke again. Or what happened. Reluctantly, I pull up the text.

But it's not Miranda. At first I don't even recognize the number.

Meet me in the Hang Out at 3 a.m. tonight.

I'll tell you everything.

Then my breath goes.

But it can't be. It's impossible.

Because that number belongs to Jade.

CHAPTER

thirty-seven

It can't be her.

Is it really her?

These thoughts bounce in my head, as I force my eyes to stay open. I don't want to miss the meeting time, in case the alarm doesn't wake me up on vibrate.

1:09 a.m.

Who could have texted me this? Who got her phone?

Bob and Joanie? They would have easy access to her phone. And maybe Bob was in debt from gambling. But I still don't see them getting staff members to threaten me.

1:55 a.m.

Maybe Bryce got the phone. He could have killed her. She definitely revealed a controlling, abusive side in her journal, and he's shown quasi-violent tendencies before. He could have consorted with the staff to shut me up, then played dumb about it. But again, I don't really see it.

2:01 a.m.

Diego still seems the most likely. She was blackmailing him. She could get him in jail. He had the most to lose. He and Sergei could have easily tossed Jade overboard and convinced the crew to threaten me.

2:17 a.m.

Could it be Jade after all?

2:23 a.m.

Caleb? No. Jade would probably kick his ass.

2:24 a.m.

Some random psychopath roaming the ship who attacked her? Maybe. Doubtful.

2:28 a.m.

Maybe she killed herself. But I squash that thought immediately. It's impossible. I'm not even considering it one for another second.

2:30 a.m.

Could it be her? Just maybe?

I look at my phone so many times, I'm afraid the battery might run out. Time crawls until finally my phone shows 2:45 a.m. After a quick check on my family, I throw on some clothes I'd left by the bedside last night, stash my key card in my pocket, and hold my phone in front of me to guide the way to the door. Then, out of nowhere . . .

Bang.

"What? What is it?" my dad yells, looking around the room in sleepy confusion. The trash can has emptied all over the floor from where I ran into it. Holding my breath, I turn off my phone.

"Ted," my mom says, her voice hoarse and tired. "What is it?"

"I thought I heard something," he says, appearing more awake now.

In my best annoyed voice, I say, "I was just going to the bathroom. Jeez."

My mom rolls onto her other side. "Go back to sleep, Ted," she says.

But he's already lightly snoring. I wait a solid twenty seconds and open the door. Whoever's on the other side of this message, it's a trap, I know it. But I have to take the chance before they hurt me, or my family.

———

The ship is dead at this time of night, the boisterous, lively atmosphere replaced with a ghost town. Scattered staff move about, washing floors, spraying tables, lugging huge bags of trash. Outside, the pool and hot tub have CLOSED, SEE YOU SOON! signs standing up like traffic cones. The hot tub burbles like a witch's cauldron, eerily empty. The mall shops are dark. One yawning staff member mans the 24-7 Caffeine Fix kiosk.

I hit the elevator button, and in seconds, an empty elevator arrives. I step in, and piped-in music plays overhead. Some upbeat jazz, totally opposite of the mood of the ship right now. The elevator stops on the next floor, but no one gets on, like a ghost pushed the button. I stand there for a moment, waiting, until the door closes. Two more flights up to the Hang Out floor. When the elevator door dings open, I step out carefully, afraid that someone might leap out and grab me. But no one does.

I exit and walk down the long hall to the Hang Out.

My mouth has gone bone-dry, but I keep walking, my heart whacking in my chest.

Finally, I reach the door. I take one last deep breath, put the key card in, and push the door.

And there he stands, looking at me with a stony gaze.

Bryce.

CHAPTER

thirty-eight

"It's you?" I say. I barely get the words out, my breath coming in spurts.

Bryce gives me a weird look. "What's me?"

"You killed Jade," I say.

Confusion flashes across his face, quickly switching to anger, his nostrils flaring. "I told you a hundred fucking times, Izzy. I didn't kill her. All right?"

"Then . . . ," I say, idiotically glancing around the room as though the killer were hiding somewhere. "What are you doing here?"

He crosses his arms. "I was going to play some video games since I can't sleep. What are *you* doing here?"

"Um . . . I . . ." I have no idea what to say. I didn't have Bryce playing video games at three a.m. on my bingo card. I glance at my phone, which says 3:03. I don't want Bryce around if the person who texted me from Jade's phone does come. They might not show if they hear two voices. Or he could get involved in something dangerous. "You probably shouldn't stay," I say.

Bryce snorts. "What, you own the Hang Out now?"

"No," I say, faltering. "It's just . . . it's hard to explain . . ."

He waits, probably for me to try. But when I don't, he shoves the console away on the table. "Forget it. I don't even want to play anymore."

"I'm sorry. I really am." I bite my lip. "I just can't tell you because . . ."

"Whatever, Izzy. Have at it. You can have the Hang Out all to yourself," he says with an exaggerated sweeping motion. He shakes his head in annoyance. "You know, I never understood what Jade saw in you anyway." Then he walks out without a backward glance.

The door closes behind him with a solid click.

I move to the beanbag and sit there, waiting. A clock with an anchor pendulum tick-tocks, the sound burrowing into my brain as minutes crawl by. I check my phone a thousand times, but there's nothing. My eyes keep shutting, even though my body feels caffeinated and restless.

I must doze off, because a half hour of unwatched times goes by. Three-forty-five a.m.

I give it another fifteen minutes and then decide to admit defeat. It was stupid to get my hopes up like that.

Maybe someone just wanted to see if I'd show up. Maybe they were spooked when Bryce was there. Maybe someone got a hold of her phone and was playing a sick joke. Either way, the result is the same. I'm sitting on a beanbag at four a.m. in the Hang Out like an idiot. I stretch out a yawn and start to stand up when a cruise-text comes onto my phone. Again, I don't recognize the number.

But the message shocks me into sitting back down.

Help!! It's Jade. Trapped me in a room. Can't get out.

I stare at my phone in disbelief.

There's no way. It can't be Jade.

Who? Where? I type back as fast as I can.

Diego. Don't know where. Storage room. Paint buckets everywhere.

I pause for a second. Talk about a trap . . . Lull me into a storage room where I'll never be seen again. *How do I know it's really you?*

Dots linger on the screen. Then two words.

Jelly Belly.

Oh my God. It's her.

Has she been on the ship all along?

My nerves jangling, I yank open the door.

And there he stands, his bulky figure blocking the door.

Before I can decide if I should run or try to force my way through, he grabs me by the neck, lifting me off the ground. I claw at the hand squeezing my throat as I'm carried back into the room. My throat burns, and I'm choking for a breath when his grip releases, dumping me unceremoniously on a beanbag. My hands fly up to my bruised neck as I start sucking in air again.

Sergei looms over me with a sneer of a smile. "Let's talk."

thirty-nine

"You really didn't think Jade was coming, did you?" Sergei mocks in his thick Russian accent.

Shrinking away from him in the beanbag, I shake my head. My throat still feels raw, and I don't know if my voice will work yet.

"Good, then you're a little smarter than you look." He squats next to me, like a teacher speaking to a child. Fumes of alcohol come off his breath. He crosses his bulging arms, his black scythe tattoo peeking from his collar. "Now, someone's been a bad girl, hasn't she?"

I don't answer.

"I gave you warning after warning. But you could not leave it alone, could you?" he asks, his jaw clenching.

I take a painful, dry swallow. "I'll drop it," I say, my voice barely audible.

Again, that leer of a smile pops on his face, "You'll what?" he asks, cupping his hand to his ear.

"Drop it," I whisper, louder.

He nods. "Yes, I think you will."

I don't like the sound of this, though. I point at the camera. "Recording us," I choke out.

"Yup," he says, pointing as well. "Hi," he says, waving at the camera. "Only, I disabled it before you came. Oops." He inches closer to me. "So sad for your friend." He lets out a theatrical sigh. Then his face brightens. "She was a pain in the ass, though, no? She took money from my friend. She was going to tell on us." He does a tsk-tsk, shaking his pointer finger. "We couldn't have that, right?" He pulls in even closer to me, revealing old acne scars pitting his face. "I'm not going to jail again. Not a nice place. Even for bad guys."

I back up, the beanbag crunching under me. "You killed her, then?"

"Close," he says. "Diego killed her. He make the problem, he make the solution. All done." He wipes his hands to demonstrate.

So Sergei doesn't know Jade's still alive. Maybe I can use that to my advantage somehow. I have to think of something. She's waiting for me.

"But then someone kept asking questions. Couldn't stop, even when we ask her nicely. So now . . . one left." He comes even closer to me, and a mixture of alcohol and cologne floods my nostrils, gagging me. He pokes a stiff finger on my chest. "You."

I back myself farther into the beanbag. "If you touch me, I'll tell him," I say, the words trembling. "I'll call him right now."

"I don't think you are calling anyone."

"My mom will, though," I say. "I told her to if I don't

come home by four o'clock," I lie. "She's probably calling him right this very minute."

Sergei narrows his eyes. He doesn't seem to believe me, but also doesn't want to chance it. "Calling who?"

I clear my dry throat. "The captain."

He lets out a laugh, clearly unimpressed with the answer. "I'm in charge here, not the captain. Sergei. I make the rules," he barks with a sense of wounded pride. "Who pays off Yvonne to give you the letter? Who makes sure you get something in your soda pop?" His voice elevates with every complaint. "Who pays the man to have a little chat with your brother? I do." He points to himself, giving me the odd impression of Tarzan. He leans casually on one elbow beside me. "Easy money," he says. "Buy drugs from Bermuda . . . sell in New York." He makes a sailing motion with his hand. "Like taking candy from baby." Then his lips twist. "That is until your little friend got her claws into Diego and screwed it all up."

He leans in closer, and I drop my head back to avoid his face. "Diego takes care of his problem," he says with that stupid little smile. "Now I take care of you."

Without warning, he rears his arm back, and I see sparks and a lightning blast of pain.

And everything goes dark.

CHAPTER

forty

Soft, warm rain wakes me up, and I realize I'm outside.

And alive.

The blaring pain in my forehead confirms this. Liquid drips from my nose, and I reach up to touch it. Maroon-black stains my palms, and it takes my addled brain another few seconds to register this as blood. The skin around my eyes itches with swelling. I breathe through my mouth, my nose a mass of snot and blood.

And yet the sky glows with stars, pinpricks in a velvet sky. The moon casts a wedge of white across the dark ocean. I stare out at the beauty of this moment, when once again my brain catches up.

You are leaning against the rails of this ship.

You are about to be pushed over.

I fight to stand up, my feet slipping on the wet wood.

"Oh," Sergei says. "You woke up. I'm sorry. It will be quick. I promise. Quick splash and you are done."

He actually does sound sorry. But I don't have time to worry about this, as his hands wrench me up the railing. I punch his arms, which probably hurts my fists more than it hurts him. It feels like punching a slab of metal.

"They'll see you," I say, deciding my wits might save me faster than my puny muscles. "They have cameras all over the ship."

"No," he explains. "No camera on this part of the ship. I know ship very well."

I swat at his face, which he easily avoids, ducking like a boxer. For all I know he is a boxer. Twisting, I manage to evade his grasp for a few seconds before he grabs me again.

"Come on, Izzy," he scolds me. *Stop being so difficult when I'm trying to kill you.*

"How will you explain it?" I ask, short of breath from fighting him. "Won't they question it? Two girls overboard?"

Sergei lets out a laugh. "Have you not heard of the curse of the *Crown Jewel*?" His meaty hand pushes against my chest, squeezing my sternum. "We make this funny story. Stupid Americans believe it." His fingers dig into my skin. "Cruise ship buries it. No one wants to talk about it. Too much money to lose." Pinning me against the railing, he slowly lifts me. "Don't fight it," he says.

I feel myself slipping over and shimmy my body, catching a glimpse of foamy black waves. The low moan of the motor vibrates against my back. Vertigo washes over me, and I flail. With one last gasp, I throw a kick, just as I've been taught in every self-defense class, right where you're supposed to kick a man.

And it lands.

Hard.

His hands drop to cradle his mashed-up privates, and I almost fall over the rail with the sudden position change. But I throw my weight forward and fall back onto the ship. I get only one step away when I'm yanked back. Sergei's eyes brim with fury. His huge hand boxes the side of my head. My ear sings in pain, a high-pitched sound drilling through my skull. I fall sideways. And I think about biology. The semicircular canals. The crystals in my ears dislodged. The biology test. Luke. *What's the worst thing you've ever done?*

I should have told my parents. I should have told Jade.

Again, I am lifted up. My head takes a nauseating spin. I claw at his face and miss. Then all at once, he grunts, and I feel myself falling.

Falling, falling.

With a solid, painful thunk . . . onto the deck. Again, my brain catches up. He didn't do it. He didn't push me over. My head spinning, I try to sit up when I see what has stopped him.

My mom stands there with a maniacal look on her face, holding my lacrosse stick. For a bizarre moment, I think she wants to practice with me. But then I understand exactly what she's doing. She javelins him in the face, and blood spurts out, black as oil.

His blood now.

And she keeps spearing him, over and over, until he finally collapses.

She stands over him then, her stick held high, looking like some warrior queen. "Are you okay?" she asks me, panting for breath.

"Yes!" I yell above the ringing in my ears. "We have to get Jade!"

CHAPTER

forty-one

The rain has picked up, thudding on the deck now.

"She's in a storage room?" my mom asks after reading the text. She sounds short of breath still, dazed and in shock. "What's Jelly Belly?"

"Never mind," I say. "If they find out I'm alive, they might kill her. We don't have much time."

"I know." My mom wipes rain off her face, streaking blood across her cheeks. I notice she's wearing rain-soaked pajamas. "There could be a million storage rooms, though."

We run into the ship, and then I think of it—the schematic by guest services. Closing my eyes, I strain to remember. Crew's quarters . . . safety equipment . . . *storage*. "Fifth deck," I say.

My voice sounds too loud in the sudden quiet of the ship. My arms shiver in the blast of air-conditioning.

"How do you know that?" my mom asks, still holding the lacrosse stick.

"I saw it," I say. "Just believe me. Let's go already."

"Okay," she says, and we both look back through the window at Sergei's body on the deck. I'm hesitant to leave him, in case he wakes up, but finding Jade is more important.

We sneak down the stairs in case someone sees us.

Every thudding step jolts my body, and my ankle is throbbing; I must have twisted it somehow. I hold on to the railing, my ribs aching.

"Come on, honey," my mom says, strength in her voice. She holds my hand. "We can do this."

I nod, and we keep going down the dank-smelling stairs. The ship gets darker and darker, lit only by dull, flickering fluorescent lights. My ankle twinges with every step. Clomp. Clomp. Clomp. We go deep into the belly of the ship, farther than I even realized we could.

"That was deck four," my mom says as we continue our descent. Then we open the heavy door to deck five.

We start running, kicking up dust. Pockmarks scar the walls, and spiderwebs hang in corners. It seems to be a forgotten area of the ship. She could be stuck down here forever. Nobody ever comes here.

"Jade!" I scream out. But the name just echoes. We keep jogging. I try to ignore the throbbing in my ankle. "Jade," I yell again, my voice hoarse.

"Shh," my mom whispers, standing stock-still. "Did you hear something?"

I stand and listen, when I hear it too, just the faintest cry. "It must be her," I say.

So we take off again, our feet thumping on the floor, calling out to her. A weak voice calls my name back, and we follow it, turning down corridors and whipping around corners. Finally we get closer until we're standing right outside of it. The door appears thick and solid, reinforced. It's a wonder we could hear her at all. "We're here," I say, and twist the knob.

Of course it's locked. For some reason, I hadn't anticipated this. Since she can't get out either, it must be a double lock. "What are we going to do?" I ask, panic setting in.

"Stay calm," my mom says, gazing around the empty hallway at mounds of dust rimming the walls, rat droppings in the corner.

"What are you looking for?" I ask, looking around too.

"A wire," she says, her eyes still searching. "I just need a wire. Do you have a bobby pin or something?"

I give her an incredulous look. "Do I *look* like I have a bobby pin?"

A distant knock sounds from the other side. "Look down," Jade says, her voice soft behind the thick door. Slowly, an unbent paper clip emerges from under the door.

My mom swipes it. "Thanks, Jade," she says. "We'll get you out. Don't worry. Just wait a minute." Snapping the paper clip in half, she drops to her knee and examines the lock, then sticks the wire in and starts jiggling. "Damn it. I used to be able to do this." Desperation runs through the words. She keeps maneuvering the wires and grunting as paper clip scrapes against metal. "I almost had it." She twists her wrist just so, and we hear a magical click. She turns the knob.

My mom pulls the hefty door open to see Jade in front of us.

Jade shields her eyes from the dim hall light. She's wearing dirty sweats, her hair snarly and greasy, her lips dry and cracked. Her pale skin is even paler now. She looks skeletal, as if she has lost even more weight. Her room smells of sweat, urine, and fear. "Thank you," she says in a hoarse, cracking voice.

"Come on, girls," my mom urges us. "We need to get the captain." We all turn around to go when a voice comes from the hallway.

"I don't think so," Diego says.

forty-two

The nose of his black gun points at us.

"Now you are all going into the naughty room," he says in a low, menacing voice. "Until we can figure out what to do with you."

With that, he shoves us back toward the room.

"No," Jade starts a weak cry. "No."

"Sergei was right. I should have killed you," he growls as he starts to shut the door.

It's now or never. I can wait until they come back and kill us or I can die trying to save us. With everything in me, I charge, darting my bony-skinny self through the little space left between Diego and the door.

"Hey!" he yells. But he's still got to lock the door before chasing after me, so I run. I hear a soft pop, and a chip off a wall whizzes by my face. I've run a few more steps before I realize it was from a bullet. He must have a silencer. Another one cracks the wall as I make a turn. I hear his footsteps now. I turn down one corridor, then another. I have no idea where I am, but maybe I can lose him.

"Izzy," he calls out, the name jeering. "Come on, Izzy. You know I'm going to catch you."

I find a stairway and open the door as softly as I can. I can't afford to take the elevator and give him time to catch up.

"Izzy!" His voice fades behind the door.

I climb for my life. Up. Up. Up. Like I'm in a lacrosse game, chasing a girl in the final seconds. Sweat pours down my face. I can't breathe through my nose.

Up. Up. Another flight. Another flight.

Every breath hurts. My ankle screams in pain.

Gasping, I finally exit on our deck. I've never been so happy to go into our stupid dungeon cell of a room. Barely breathing, I insert the key and throw open the door.

"Dad!" I yell.

But instead, I see the captain standing there, looking around the room. "Izzy," he says, seeing me. His expression morphs into shock. "What's going on? Are you hurt?" He hurries out of the room.

"Where's my dad? Where's Trey?" I ask, catching my breath.

He shakes his head in confusion. "That's what I'm trying to find out. We found Sergei, who said your mom attacked him. Then we got a report that your dad and brother were seen wandering the ship." His eyebrows scrunch in worry. "I'm assuming Sergei didn't tell me the whole story."

"No," I say, grabbing his arm. "He attacked me, and my mom saved me." The words tumble out as I catch my breath. "It was like I told you. Sergei told me about the drug smuggling." I squeeze his arm even harder. "But now Diego has Jade and my mom."

"Whoa," he says, backing up, the pink imprint of my fingers on his forearm. "You're saying Jade is alive?"

"Yes," I squeal, impatient. "Diego locked them all up in a storage room. We need to get them."

"Okay, okay," he says. He stares straight ahead, appearing to be concentrating, maybe running through scenarios. "Okay," he repeats, this time in a take-charge manner. "Hostage situation." He shifts his gaze back to me. "Here's what we're going to do. We're going to contact security and take care of Diego. And your father and brother may be in danger too."

Briskly, he walks ahead, and I follow. "We need to get to my quarters. Apprise Sven of the situation." He turns to me as we walk. "I'm so sorry that I didn't believe you, Izzy." He bites his lip. "I put you and your family in danger. And that's my fault. But we're taking care of that right now. We'll get the coast guard involved too."

Walking with him, I finally start to relax, just a touch. Someone is finally helping me. The cavalry is coming. My family will be safe. Jade will be safe. And I won't have to worry about Diego or Sergei anymore.

Then his radio squawks with static and we both stop dead.

"I've secured two of the targets. Still looking for the girl . . . copy."

We stare at each other. The captain's mouth drops open, his eyes flashing with panic. And I realize whose voice was on the radio.

Diego.

"Izzy," he says, putting up his hands. "It's not how it looks."

I surge ahead of him, and he immediately chases after me. I'm running, though I don't even know where I'm running to. Sergei wasn't running the show, even if he wanted to believe it. Here I am, feeding him information while he plays the role of a boorish, bumbling idiot. And I fell right for it.

"Izzy!" the captain yells, gaining ground on me. His fingers swipe my hair. "Izzy!" he screams again.

But then I see my dad down the hall, near the captain's quarters, with Trey bouncing in his arms. "Izzy?" he calls out, his eyes popping with alarm. "What happened to you? Where's your mom?"

"ZiZi has boo-boos," Trey says, appearing stricken.

"Yes, and I was just helping her," the captain says in his usual casual, friendly way, now right behind me.

"He's lying!" I yell, dashing ahead. "They've got Mom. And Jade."

"Izzy slipped and hurt herself," the captain says, taking calm strides. "She's not making a lot of sense right now."

I throw myself behind my dad. "He's lying, Dad. He was chasing me. I swear to you."

They measure each other a moment; then, "Captain," Trey says with excitement, recognizing him from the tour. "Push the button? Please?"

Trey wriggles out of my dad's arms and takes off. And I follow. I hear pushing and shoving behind us. Someone thuds against the wall. A punch hits flesh.

"The button!" Trey yells with joy.

"Yes, but we have to run!" I say with energy, trying to sound playful. I hope my dad is able to hold back the captain. "The bad guys are coming!"

"I run," he squeals, laughing. "I run!"

The captain's quarters are straight ahead. I pound on the door with all my might. Sven peers through the window with a questioning look.

"You okay?" he asks, squinting at my face.

"Please," I cry, knocking. "Let us in."

He opens the door, and we rush in. And to his utter bewilderment, Trey scrambles over to the control area and slams the red button.

"What are you doing?" Sven asks with horror.

Trey grins. "We hit the button."

CHAPTER

forty-three

The cavalry arrives.

Sven explained the situation to the command center, and within ten minutes, the ship fills with controlled chaos as coast guard and Navy SEALs file in and take over. Helicopters rock the air above us, lowering more soldiers onto the vessel.

In tactical positions around the ship, they stand with guns raised, barking out orders. Loud, official announcements come over the speakers, announcing that passengers should stay in their rooms, and everyone else should shelter in place.

In shock, we all huddle in the officers' quarters—Sven, my dad, Trey, and me. A serious-faced woman barges into the room in blue camo. The tag on one pocket reads "Coast Guard," the other "Kane," which must be her name. "All right. Who's in charge here?"

"Staff Captain," Sven says, standing tall. "Lieutenant Sven." Glancing at her epaulets, he adds "Ma'am" with a salute.

"At ease, lieutenant," she says. "And this is the Mathers family?"

"Yes," he answers.

"Touch the gun?" Trey asks, looking up at me with hope in his eyes.

"No, shush," I whisper as Kane throws him an amused glance.

"Okay," she says in a no-nonsense voice. "As I understand it, we've got an alleged drug smuggling operation, multiple offenders on the ship."

"Yes," Sven says, sounding a bit sheepish. "I'm . . . I'm just learning of this."

She gives a staunch nod. Crackling comes over her radio. "Kane, copy."

"Copy. Captain and coconspirators in custody. Hostages have been accounted for and are—"

The door bursts open then, along with another blue camo soldier accompanying my mom and Jade.

"Here, it appears," Kane says, smiling for the first time.

Crying, my mom runs over to hug me, then my father and Trey. "Ew," Trey complains. "Mom all wet." There is a burst of laughter and more hugging as Kane pushes the button on her radio again, dashing off more orders.

"I push the button?" Trey asks, gazing at the radio.

"Shush," I say again, but Kane grins.

"Sure, buddy. You can push it." She removes the radio. "Let me show you what to do."

I put a weak arm around Jade, and she gives me a wry smile, the old Jade peeking through. "You look like crap," she says.

"Same," I tell her.

I start to laugh, but she grabs me in a tight hug, so tight

I can hardly breathe, crushing my bruised ribs. Hugging her back, I feel her body rocking against me, and realize that she's sobbing, wet tears soaking onto my shoulder.

"It's okay," I say, patting her back, like a mother might, as she cries on my shoulder. "It's gonna be okay."

CHAPTER

forty-four

DAY 14

Arrival in New York City

We're bruised and battered, but alive.

My face looks awful, but it's no worse than when I got smacked in the face by an overzealous field hockey player. Other than a bruised neck, a mashed-up face, and a couple other bumps, I'm alive. And thankfully, so is Jade.

After a long debriefing by the coast guard on our last day on the ship, we finally dock in New York City. The *Crown Jewel* offered our family and Jade's family an overnight stay at the Four Seasons, an obvious ploy to hold off any pending lawsuits. Bob and Joanie had the grace to go back to New Jersey for now and leave Jade with us, until they figure things out for Jade.

We check in at the front desk in the ridiculously posh lobby. My feet touch the solid, veined marble floor, but I feel like I'm still moving on the sea.

"I'm hungry," Trey whines. Having heard this complaint

a hundred times already, I tune him out. "Hungry," Trey repeats, poking my hip this time for emphasis.

"Ow," I say as he catches the bruise from my scuffle with Sergei.

My dad pulls Trey in toward him, putting his hands on his shoulders. My dad has a good shiner too from his fight with the captain, where he managed to hold him back just long enough for us to get to the button. "Don't bother your sister," he scolds.

"I'm hungry," Trey says louder, in case we didn't hear him.

"We're all checked in," my mom announces, striding back from the front desk.

Trey decides to lie on the floor.

My parents look at each other and sigh. "You girls want to explore?" my mom asks.

Jade shrugs. "I was thinking maybe a carriage ride?"

———

We didn't count on the horse jostling every sore bone in our bodies or the damp, unseasonably cold weather, but with the soft smell of horse and flannel blanket around us, we relax into the carriage ride. Molly (the horse) clomps around the city while the driver tries to tell us about landmarks. Jade and I don't speak for some time. We haven't yet, very much. It seems almost like there is too much to say.

Finally, I break the silence.

"I read your journal," I say, unsure why I even decided to share this.

She turns to me with surprise. "You did?"

I catch a hint of accusation in her tone. "Yeah," I admit. "That's how I found out about everything." The driver makes a clicking sound, and the carriage rocks forward again.

"Huh," she says. I'm wondering if she's thinking about the private things, too, how her uncle gambles, how she's still a virgin. How Bryce hated me.

"Someone took it, though. I don't have it anymore." I pull the blanket farther over us as a breeze shoots through the carriage. "Sorry," I say.

"Don't be," she says, then lets out a tired laugh. "You kind of saved my life . . . so . . . I think we can call it even."

"Okay," I say, smiling too.

We don't speak again, the rhythmic clacking of the hooves filling the air. Traffic whirs all around us, honking everywhere.

"Did he hurt you?" I ask, then want to kick myself for prying. She would have told me already if she wanted to. "You don't have to say anything—"

"No," she says. "It's okay." She takes a deep breath. The sunlight shows dark rings under her eyes. "I was scared . . . really scared. But he didn't hurt me or rape me or anything." She snuggles into the blanket. "I suppose I should be thankful. I mean, he could have just killed me, but . . ." Her eyebrows lower in a thoughtful expression. "It was almost like he wanted to keep me for himself. Like a pet." She gives a disgusted headshake. "But the truth is, I was scared that he might . . . not let me go after all. Maybe just leave me there to die."

"You ladies comfortable back there?" the driver asks,

making us jump. He smiles with the reins in his hands, his cheeks ruddy.

"Yup," we both answer, and he nods and faces forward again.

"I've been meaning to ask you," I say, blowing on my hands. "If you were there the whole time, then . . . how did your bloody clothes wash ashore?"

"His blood," she says. "He cut his arm and showed me. I think it was like a threat. Like, *don't think I won't cut you too.*" She shifts in the seat as the horse whinnies at something. "But he wanted it to look like I was dead, so people wouldn't try to find me. And so he wouldn't get in trouble with Sergei." The horse whinnies again, streams of fog coming out of her nostrils. "I suppose it was just lucky for him that they actually washed up on shore.

"Hey," she says, blowing on her pink hands too. "Whatever happened with Luke?"

"Oh," I say, with a shrug. "He dumped me. Cheated with some skank."

"No shit," she says, looking wronged on my behalf.

"And put it on Insta," I add.

The horse sways while we stop in traffic. Jade shakes her head with a rueful look. "Men suck," she says simply.

"Pretty much," I agree, and the clomping starts up again. "Speaking of which," I say, "what about Bryce? You guys staying together?"

She gives an incredulous laugh. "No way."

I lean against her, and we just sit for a bit, breathing in the cold air, the scent of hay, and street pretzels. The salty ocean air seems a distant memory. "Would you ever go on a cruise again?" I ask.

"Are you nuts?" she asks, turning and laughing.

"Yeah, that's what I was thinking."

"Although . . . ," she says, yawning. "I have always wanted to go to Alaska. That sounds kind of cool."

"Yeah," I admit. "It does." I lean back in the carriage booth, feeling like all is right in the world, until I see Jade staring out at the cityscape with a troubled look.

"What is it?" I ask.

"I left something on the ship," she says in a small voice. "Something I really needed." Her eyes don't move from their spot in the distance.

"It's not there," I answer, and she turns to me in question, her eyes light blue in the sunlight. "The money?" I ask. "In the safe?"

She answers with a hesitant nod.

"Gone," I say. "I think the captain took it." I toy with the blanket. "Probably in the evidence room. With your phone."

She stares out again and doesn't say anything for a bit. "I know I shouldn't have done it. Blackmailed him. It was stupid. But . . . I just wanted to get an apartment, you know? For my mom."

I think of what Bob and Joanie said, how she blamed herself for telling on her mom and how she was trying to make it up. But she shouldn't have to do that. A sixteen-year-old shouldn't have to try to raise her mother.

"You know how you asked me what the worst thing I ever did was?"

240

Jade nods, yawning again. "You stole lipstick."

I take a deep breath. "I lied," I say. "I cheated. On a big biology test. Gave Luke all the answers."

"Oh," Jade says, stretching out the word.

"Yeah," I say.

"And then he goes and cheats on you," she says, wincing.

"Yeah," I repeat. "Nice, huh." Gently, I scratch my sore chin. "I might get kicked out of school. Which means I'll never get into college. *And* I haven't even told my parents yet."

"Oh," she says again, drawing the word out even longer this time. "They're probably going to kill you."

"Yeah, probably. Since Sergei didn't manage it." Then I chuckle. "I suppose if I can handle Sergei, I can handle telling my parents, right?"

"I know you," she says. "You'll figure it out." Then we both turn forward, watching the driver gently bouncing in his seat, the reins swaying in his hands. Again, I feel bad for Jade. At least my parents are there, and they care. At least they *want* to kill me. We're quiet for a while, just listening to the buzz of the city and the clomping on the street.

"Thanks, Izzy," Jade says quietly.

"For what?" I ask.

"For not giving up on me," she says.

CHAPTER

forty-five

After about a million hugs, we finally go our separate ways.

We have each other's phone numbers, with a plan to get together for Thanksgiving. Until then, we can always go old-school FaceTime. After we settle Jade into a cab taking her to her gram's house, my dad hails a taxi for us.

My family scoots into the seat, inhaling the cloying scent of strawberry air freshener. My dad takes his usual seat in the front, next to the driver, and the rest of us squeeze into the back.

As we pull away from the hotel, I get a sense of hurtling toward a black hole. Vacation is over. School will swallow me up again. Luke will be there, too. And I can't avoid it anymore. Soon enough, they will know. They will know everything and—

"Mom," I say. "I have something to tell you."

She looks at me and takes off her readers, folding up the cruise bill. "Okay?"

I wait for a second, to get the words ready, my stomach crawling with nerves. "I'm in trouble . . . at school."

Her face takes on a questioning cast. "What do you mean?"

I can see my father straining to listen from the front seat. I stare down at the scuffed floor mat, wanting to vomit. "I cheated. Um, with Luke." I don't dare to look up from the floor. "I gave him the answers on a biology test and now I . . . well . . ." I take in a quick breath. "I think I might get kicked out."

My mom doesn't speak. The silence stretches between us, worse than any reprimand. My father is silent up front as well, until finally my mom says, "I know."

I let out a shocked gasp. "You know?"

She nods slowly and reaches across Trey to give my knee a little squeeze. "We got an email from your teacher a couple days ago. He found out what happened."

"But we wanted *you* to tell us," my dad says, half turning from behind the plastic partition.

She sighs. "I know you work hard. And you're a good kid. But . . . you made a mistake. You definitely made a mistake on this one."

I swallow a painful lump. I really don't want to start crying in the taxicab. "Yeah," I squeak out.

"And I'm sure that Luke had some role in all this anyway," she mutters.

"That Luke" raises my hackles, but it's true. "That's over anyway. He's with . . . another girl."

My mom puts her glasses in her purse. "So, when we get back to school, we'll meet with your teacher, and we'll see what happens. If you get suspended, or even expelled, we'll deal with it," she says, putting on a brave face. She squeezes my knee again. "And we'll try to put this all behind us. Okay?"

I let out a shaky breath of relief. "Okay." I guess after almost getting killed, cheating seems less consequential.

"Anyway, we'll work out your punishment. And you'll be happy to know we're not planning on taking another cruise for a while."

"Oh," I say, tapping my foot on the floor. "Jade and I were actually thinking about doing an Alaskan cruise."

My dad swivels his head to me with an amused look. "Alaska?"

"Alaska!" Trey yells out, turning from the window. "Alaska! Alaska!"

I don't think he even knows what the word means. "Just a thought," I say.

My mom tilts her head. "I *have* always wanted to see the icebergs calving. If it isn't too expensive . . ." She seems to consider it a minute, but then sits up straight, perhaps realizing that I'm trying to distract her from the whole cheating and punishment thing. "We'll think about Alaska. But as for the cheating, unfortunately, there are consequences." Her stern mom face comes back on. "No phone for two weeks. And you're grounded for one month. Except for after-school activities."

At that point, I may have accidentally rolled my eyes.

"Listen," she says, her voice taking on a lecturing tone. And we all know what that means. One must do the opposite, for the sake of self-preservation. So I sneak in my earbuds and turn on my music. My gaze shifts out the window, past the bodegas, the cafés, and the throngs of people crowding the sidewalks with billboards overhead. In my mind, though, I still see miles of blue water. I still feel the sway of the ship as the music rolls over me.

Like an ocean wave.

Acknowledgments

First off, thank you, Rachel, for putting this project in my lap. It went from "By the way, do you have any YA thriller ideas?" to a phone call announcing a deal a couple of weeks later. It sounds like an inspirational poster, but sometimes the best things happen when you least expect them.

Thank you, Wendy Loggia and Hannah Hill, for taking this cruise with me (okay, okay . . . sorry!). Hannah, your insights made the book immeasurably better. Thank you, Casey Moses and Sophia Chunn, for the stunning cover! And thank you, Beverly Horowitz, Tamar Schwartz, Colleen Fellingham, Jen Valero, Caitlyn Whalen, Emma Benshoff, Kelly McGauley, Kate Keating, Elizabeth Ward, John Adamo, and Dominique Cimina for working to put this baby out into the world!

Thank you to Deb Shapiro for championing the book with us.

Thanks to the Tall Poppies for their love and support, and for letting me back into the fold.

Thanks to my Physician Writing Peeps, who get what it means to both doctor and write.

Thank you to my parents, my biggest cheerleaders always! Any similarity to actual persons or events is purely coincidental. . . .

Thank you to Margie Long for stocking the Canterbury shelves with my books, even if someone always steals them.

Thank you to my husband for not killing me for skipping the IUP family football game to write. And for further not killing me when I continued to write the entire ride home so you could keep up the conversation. Any grammatical mistakes are mine.

Thank you to my kids, who are becoming actual mature adults.

Every year is an adventure, and I am privileged to spend them all with you.

About the Author

Sandra Block graduated from college at Harvard, then returned to her native land of Buffalo, New York, for medical training and never left. She is a practicing neurologist and proud Sabres fan, and lives at home with her husband, two children, and impetuous yellow lab. She is the author of the acclaimed thrillers *Little Black Lies, The Girl Without a Name, The Secret Room,* and *What Happened That Night. Girl Overboard* is her first novel for teens.

sandraablock.com